# Trouble IN-LAW

SALLY CLEMENTS

**ISBN:** 9798449289124

# Chapter One

"Tell me you're not." Louise Bennett wove between the tables in *Precious Things*, piled high with scented candles, vases, crystal glasses, wrapped French soaps, and precariously balanced rose-printed teacups, and gaped at her friend. "It's June. Who the hell writes Christmas cards in June?"

"I think the answer to that question is pretty obvious." Ella Blackstone picked a new card from the pile before her, opened it, and flicked to the next card on her Rolodex. "Someone who wants to make sure she has everything done before her daughter comes home for the summer."

Louise handed over two take-out cups of coffee, divested herself of her bag, and shimmied out of her jacket. "Seriously?" She frowned and chewed her lip. She opened her mouth, then closed it again as though reconsidering a decision to criticize. "You need to get a life. Leave that. Come have coffee with me." She moved to the plush sofa—part of the shop's stock, but something they would both be devastated to see sell—uncapped her coffee and discarded the lid on the glass-topped coffee table.

Ella ripped a couple of sheets off a roll of kitchen paper and picked up two coasters from the corner of her desk. It didn't seem to matter how many times she asked; Louise never used a coaster. She picked up the litter bin and brought it to their regular seating place just as she did every morning, tossed the discarded lid into it, and checked the coffee table for a damp spot. There wasn't one. She put a coaster under Louise's cup, placed one under her own, and discarded the lid into the bin.

She folded the kitchen paper into a perfect square and placed it carefully on the table. Being anally retentive was more than a pastime; it was a fact of her life. A life that began every morning with the same routine. Coffee and a croissant eaten alone at the kitchen island, then into the car for the quick drive to *Precious Things*. Every time she turned the bend in the road to see the store set back on the hillside with its long glass windows glimmering in the sunshine, she smiled. It was a survivor from another age, with tall, white columns framing the door, and a hand-painted sign in blue and gold. Inside, the vintage vibe continued. The store had been in her family since the 1950s, and had barely changed.

Dark, polished tongue and groove floorboards were covered with richly-colored rugs, and a vase of flowers graced the reception desk next to a modern cash register. In a previous life, the place had been an upmarket jewelry store with long display cases full of priceless diamond, sapphire, ruby and emerald rings. There had been another room, where private clients were invited to view the most exclusive stock by appointment.

When Ella took over, she'd knocked these two rooms into one huge showroom, and filled it with furniture, pictures, ornaments, and rugs, making the entire space open and inviting. There was still a small private office in the back, but Ella and Louise preferred to be 'front of house.' They could gaze from the full-length windows to the parking lot, and see the changing seasons from the sofa. The warm and inviting atmosphere they'd worked hard to create had earned them enthusiastic repeat customers, who always checked out *Precious Things* when they needed the perfect present.

"Are you going to take off your shades?" Ella asked. "Because wearing them inside is way too Hollywood for morning."

"After caffeine." Louise slid the sunglasses down her nose and peeked over them with bloodshot eyes. "I'm suffering."

"How did last night go?"

Louise grimaced. "The next time I decide to do body shots with a thirty-year-old stud, for god's sake, stop me."

"I will. And I would have if you'd told me your hot date was that young. I'd need to save you from yourself!" She usually declined when asked to join her friend at a bar. She'd said no so often Louise had stopped asking. It had been months since the divorce; her default answer was 'not tonight'. Maybe...

"Would you have come?" Before Ella had a chance to reply, Louise continued. "You always say you're too busy. But honey, I hate to tell you, you can't be that busy if you're writing Christmas cards in June."

"I can't socialize. I don't know how to act around men anymore. I don't know what to say."

Louise blew out a breath. "I don't go out to get a man. I go out because meeting people is a hell of a lot more fun than staying in talking to my cat. I'm going to Alison's art gallery opening on Thursday. Will you come with me?"

"Yes. I will." It was time to stop being such a coward.

Louise drained her coffee. Grinned. "Good."

"I've almost finished the Christmas cards. I'll get them done while the shop is quiet." Ella discarded their empty coffee cups, walked back to the desk, and started writing.

Louise followed. "Have we heard anything from Pashmina Chris?" She sat and opened her laptop.

"He emailed to say he'd be bringing the new stock over tomorrow." Ella tucked her hair behind her ears, slid a Christmas card into an envelope, and started writing.

"You know he could just courier them over." There was a teasing note in Louise's voice. "And he sure doesn't come here to see me."

Their pashmina supplier was a silver fox looking for a vixen, and for some obscure reason, he'd set his sights on Ella. Three times he'd asked her out. Three times she said no. "I think by now he must have got the message that I'm not interested."

"I don't know why you aren't. He's fun. I'd go out with him if he asked me. You should live a little. Get out of your comfort zone and go on a couple of dates. What do you have to lose?"

Her eyes narrowed at some sight out of the window. "Fuckity fuck. Shit alert."

Ella looked up. There was only one person Louise could be referring to, and right enough, there he was. Jason Blackstone. The man who believed the sun rose in the sky every morning for the sole purpose of warming his treacherous bones. It was a delusion she'd supported for nineteen years, but no longer.

Said sun illuminated Jason as he strode to the door, confidence radiating from his every pore.

Ella shot a glance at the back door, but it was too late; he'd seen her. As their gazes met, he beamed his shit-eating grin, placed one tanned hand on the front door, and pushed.

She shoved her day-diary on top of the cards and stood.

"Ella." He walked across the store, ignoring Louise entirely. "Great to see you; it's been too long."

No, it hadn't. It hadn't been nearly long enough. Ella plastered on her polite expression. She rounded the desk before he got there in a desperate attempt to stop him from sitting down opposite her. "Jason. What brings you here?"

His smile faltered.

"Hi, Jason," Louise called from her position on the couch. She was giving Ella a chance to get herself together when faced with the unbearable idiot who had been her husband.

"Louise." He nodded her direction, then refocused on Ella. "I thought I'd come and see how things are going in the shop." He glanced around. "It looks great. Business good?"

"Fine." How her business was doing was none of his frickin' business. She'd started it with Louise five years ago, after inheriting the building from her grandmother.

Louise walked over, took the chair opposite Ella's and started to look busy on her laptop.

Jason's gaze flicked to Louise. He leaned close to Ella. "Can we talk?" His tone was low, conspiratorial. "In private?"

"We're swamped." Hopefully, he couldn't see the stack of Christmas cards behind her on the desktop. "I'm sure anything you want to say, you can say in front of Louise."

Louise leaned back on her chair and surveyed them both.

"It would be better said in private. Maybe we can talk in the office." He stood his ground. The muscle that constantly twitched in his jaw when he gritted his teeth pulsed like a beacon.

Being stuck in the close confines of the back office with Jason wasn't an attractive option. There was barely enough space for two people in there. "I'll give you five; man the phones for a while?"

Louise tucked a lock of hair behind her ear. "I have to collect the consignment of candlesticks at ten. If you're still talking to Jason, I'll just go."

"Fine."

His hand hovered near the base of her spine as she walked

past, but Ella increased the pace so it had no chance of connecting. The days of allowing Jason to touch her were long gone.

Once out in the fresh air, she turned to him. "So? What's so important you decided to come here?" Invading my space, breathing my air. God, how did other divorced couples manage to be civil? Not sneering at him took everything she had.

"I need money."

Ella blinked. "What?"

"You inherited the building while we were together. Half of the business is legally mi—"

Ella held up both of her hands, palms out as if pushing him away. "Wait one cotton-picking minute. You..." She pulled in a ragged breath. "You have no right to my business. Our lawyers discussed this during the settlement. This was all agreed, Jason."

He swallowed. He plastered on his best placatory smile. "You're right. I don't want the business. Of course, the business is yours. Even if my new legal representation tells me that I may have been too generous in agreeing to that." He leaned against the low wall outside *Precious Things*. "One thing both of our attorneys agreed on was this building." He stared up at the facade. The hand-lettered painted sign in blue and gold. The striped awning with a ruffled edge, which shifted in the light breeze blowing off the ocean.

Ella felt sick. "You can't."

He pulled out a long thin, folded piece of paper and proffered it.

Ella crossed her arms. "No."

"I brought you a copy of the paperwork for you to review. It says we own this building jointly, and if one of us wants or needs to sell, we can do so after giving the other party three months' notice. I'm not trying to destroy your business, but I need to liquidate some of my assets. I need money. Betsy and I—"

"Your girlfriend has something to do with this?"

He stopped, and the smile slid from his face like butter off hot toast.

"Your twenty-five-year-old girlfriend wants you to sell?"

"It's not her decision; it's mine." He stared pointedly into the shop. "We need to get the realtor in to value the premises, and maybe Louise can buy me out. Maybe your family...." He waved the paper in front of her. "I'm sorry, okay? I don't want to do this, but I don't have any other option."

She snatched the sheaf of papers. "Get lost and don't come back."

"Three months. My people will be in touch. If you haven't raised the money by then, we'll have to put *Precious Things* on the market." Jason pushed off the wall and walked away. The beam of sunlight that had been following him when he arrived hid behind the nearest cloud.

* * *

"Now you, *you* spark joy."

Ella held out the faded black, vintage tee-shirt at arm's length. The image on the front was washed-out. The seams showed signs of wear, but that was to be expected, considering its age. She pulled it close and buried her nose in the soft cotton.

"You're a keeper." She carefully folded the tour tee-shirt so the images of Ricky Martin were face-up, and placed it on the wooden chair beside the dressing table.

Then she turned to the massive mound of clothes piled high on her new double bed and sighed. Maybe this was one of those jobs she should have put off for another day.

No. She'd been delaying things for months. For six long

months, she'd hidden out in the beach house, surrounded by the boxed detritus of her old life. She'd unpacked what she needed, but the stacks of boxes in the spare room had been a silent reminder of how things used to be—the life she used to have.

This was a three-bedroom house. She didn't need the stuff; she needed the space.

And in a week, Amber would be home. This clear-out had to happen and had to happen now.

The doorbell rang.

Louise stood on the doorstep clutching a paper bag. "I brought Danish."

Ella swung the door wide. "Enter." She walked into the kitchen, found a couple of plates, and took down two mugs. "Thank god you're here. You're saving me from a fate worse than death."

Louise picked at a corner of one of the pastries. "I'm only in and out. I came to borrow a jacket."

"Hot date?"

"Just drinks. I'm meeting the sexiest man I've met all year in less than an hour, and I wanted to borrow your navy jacket with the orange trim."

"The leather one?"

Louise nodded. "What's this fate worse than death I'm not saving you from?"

"You'd be proud of me. I'm sorting my life out. I decided it was time to go through all the boxes."

"Wow." Louise sipped the cup of black coffee Ella placed in front of her. "That's brave."

"Wait until you see it. Nightmare." Ella sat opposite her friend at the breakfast bar.

"Good on you. It's about time." She pointed to a small, battered notebook Ella had left open on the table. Multicolored writing filled the pages, and pictures had been stuck in and doodled around. "Is that something you found?"

Ella grinned. She picked up the book and leafed through it. "Yes. It was one of my journals from college before I got dragged away. Full of all my hopes and dreams. I was looking through it last night, remembering. I had such plans. It's depressing to realize I didn't get to fulfill any of them."

"Like what?"

Ella flicked open a page and showed Louise.

"Places to visit: Paris, Rome, Berlin, Venice. Things to do: ride a camel through dunes, visit the pyramids, join a dig, skydive—"

"Seriously? You?" Louise's eyes widened. "I wouldn't have thought you'd be into all that stuff. I know you love history and artisan crafts, but I didn't know you had all those ambitions to see more of Europe. You didn't get a chance, did you?"

Ella shook her head. "I guess I missed my moment. I settled down so young, and once Amber came along, well, it never seemed to be the right time."

"And Jason. I can't imagine him in a foreign country."

"He never saw the point. He couldn't even see why Amber would want to go to college in Ireland. He went along with it because someone else was picking up the tab."

They sat in silence for a moment. Once again, the mere thought of Jason had soured the mood. She needed to talk to Louise about his ultimatum but hadn't yet found the words.

Louise looked around. "You finished painting. The place looks great."

When Ella bought the beach house a few months ago, the rooms were pale coral. It was inoffensive but not particularly pleasant. Over the past couple of weeks, she'd spent every evening and day she wasn't working painting it white. Now the art she'd hung popped against the fresh, clean walls. And the rugs scattered over the warm wooden floorboards looked inviting.

"I wanted a fresh start. Something that's just me. Jason always loved strong colors on the walls. He hated white or magnolia paint with a vengeance. I think with a view like that; I want white." The view was indeed spectacular.

There was a stretch of manicured green lawn, then a white picket fence beyond which the pale sand led down to the azure water.

"I've settled in, but Amber barely spent any time here before she went to college. I painted her room, too. She can choose how to decorate when she gets here."

"When's she arriving?"

"I don't know yet. I sent the airfare, but we keep missing each other's calls with the difference in time zones. It will be soon, though. I can't wait to see her."

"I know." They sat in companionable silence for a few minutes, facing the view while drinking coffee and eating pastries.

Then Ella sighed. "Well, if you have a hot date, we better find this jacket." She walked into the bedroom.

Louise stopped in the doorway, eyes wide as she took in the Everest of clothing. "Wow. You didn't just decide to hang them in the closet?"

Ella shook her head. She rooted around in the pile, found the jacket Louise wanted and tossed it over. "In the past six months, I haven't needed any of these things. Looking at them now just makes me realize I'm not this person anymore. I'm working out what I want to keep. The rest are destined for either charity or to one of those second-hand clothes resellers."

"Second-hand Rose is good. I'll send you a link." Louise examined the jacket. She slipped it on and did a twirl. "What do you think?"

"It's perfect with that dress. Don't bother bringing it back."

"Oh no, come on. You love this jacket."

"I used to love that jacket. Jason bought it for my birthday last year. But now I just keep thinking that he bought me an expensive present to hide his affair. Bloody Betsy admired it at my birthday party, and a look passed between them. At the time, I thought she'd helped him choose it, but now I think he probably just sent her out to buy me something expensive."

"As if it wasn't bad enough that he was fooling around with his secretary...to invite her to the party and have her buy your birthday present." Louise snorted. "He's a total shit." She took Ella's arm. "I'll bring it back. You can sell it."

"No. You keep it. It looked great on me, and looks equally good on you. It's yours."

Louise's attention was on the bed. "What's this?" She picked up a silky silver top, holding it by the thin spaghetti straps that went over the shoulders and across the back. "This is very retro."

"I've had that forever." It was impossible not to smile at the memories the top brought to life. "It drapes at the front and this long bit...."

"A handkerchief hem. I remember. I had a couple of dresses that had them. Dresses I've long since donated. I guess this is a go?"

"No way." Ella scanned the clothes and picked out a dark rose mini skirt with a flippy flared hem. "It goes with this. Perfect for dancing."

"Well, okay then. I guess you need your dancing clothes." She glanced at her watch. "Shoot, I have to go."

* * *

Ella paid off the cab and strode—in as much as it is possible to stride wrapped like an Egyptian mummy in a bandage dress—into Alison Carthage's new art gallery, *Carthago*.

Louise saw her from across the room, grabbed a glass of red from a passing server, and dashed over. She looked Ella over, head to toe. "Now that's what I call a definite improvement. New shoes, too?"

"Of course." She'd cleared five rubbish sacks of clothing from the mountain on her mattress, not just the dresses that she couldn't bear to wear again, but also the matching shoes and handbags. She had carefully bagged them up as matching sets. The owner of Second-Hand Rose, a permanently exhausted woman called Rose who definitely didn't buy any of her own designer stock, had taken them in with eyes wide in amazement at the careful packaging. She'd even asked if Ella were sure she wanted to part with her entire wardrobe, but there'd been no doubt in Ella's mind. They had to go—all of them.

Half an hour later, and hundreds of dollars richer, she'd bought a vintage Herve Leger bandage dress before leaving. A quick dash into a bougie shoe store, and she'd scored a perfect pair of caged dress sandals and a studded clutch to match.

She looked good. And more than that, she felt good.

"You look great, too." She cast an appreciative eye over Louise's outfit. "New?"

"Newish." She pulled Ella to one side and whispered, "Pashmina Chris is here. Don't look now, but he's coming over."

Ella squashed the urge to turn around, but she didn't have long to wait. In mere moments he was at her shoulder.

"Wow, sexy lady." He shot Louise a glance, too. "Sexy ladies."

The words were cheesy, but somehow he managed to deliver them in a way that skirted cringeworthy.

"Oh, there's Gino. I better go say hello." With a bullshit excuse and a subtle wink, Louise made her escape, leaving Ella alone with Chris.

"When are you going to put me out of my misery and come on a date with me?"

Most of the single women here would jump at the chance of an evening with the Clooney lookalike, but somehow his chiseled features and practiced charm failed to elicit even the vaguest spark in Ella. "I'm not ready to date. As you know, I'm just divorced...."

"Six months ago," Chris reminded her. "And I'm only asking you out for a meal, not making a lifetime commitment."

"I know." God, this was so difficult. She didn't want to be a total bitch and blow him off, but no matter how politely she rejected Chris, he bounced right back, like a goddamn boomerang.

"As friends. We could go out as friends." But the way his gaze swept the curves displayed in her dress certainly looked more than friendly. "No pressure. I mean it."

"Well, as friends then. Yes. Maybe we could go out for lunch sometime."

His perfect nose wrinkled. "I was thinking more dinner, but I'll take what I can get. Lunch then. Shall we make a date for next week? Tuesday?"

"Sure. That sounds good." She looked over at Louise, making save-me eyes.

Louise waved and called her name through the throng of people milling around looking at the art.

"I think Louise needs me. See you later."

Louise was talking to the new gallery's owner, Alison, a mutual friend.

Alison leaned close. A twinkle in her eye telegraphed that

both of her friends had been more than interested in seeing her talking to Chris. "Did you give in?"

"I'm going to lunch with him on Tuesday."

Louise grinned. "That's more like it. Dinner would be better but—"

"Baby steps." Alison squeezed Ella's upper arm. "Good. One thing at a time. No pressure."

No pressure? Already Ella regretted her decision. He'd made it clear he found her attractive, but dating nowadays meant jumping into the sack at some stage. And she sure wasn't ready for that. Maybe she'd never be prepared for that.

"You're grimacing." Alison frowned. "It's not such a big deal, going for lunch with a guy. You need to get out there. You're forty, not ninety. Life has more to offer than a solitary life. And besides, you should show that bastard that there's life in the old gal yet."

"Less of the old gal." Ella glanced around the gallery, noting the artwork tastefully displayed on the walls. "All the paintings look fabulous."

"Aren't they great?" Alison's face shone at the realization of a lifelong dream. "Come have a closer look."

They lost Louise on the way to a good-looking bachelor who engaged her in conversation. On the wall before them hung a selection of seascapes—crystal clear water swirling in endless shades of green and blue. Ella sighed. "Michael's work is so beautiful." Tiny red dots graced the small white cards next to each picture. "And he's selling!" She darted a look at Alison. "Are all those stickers from today?"

Alison nodded with a grin.

"I'm so happy for him. For all of your artists." Three artists exhibiting at Alison's gallery had previously displayed their work for sale at *Precious Things*. Looking around, Ella noticed red stickers on many of their pieces, too.

"You did the right thing, introducing us." Alison patted

Ella's arm. "I couldn't believe you were introducing your artists to the competition, but I'm glad you did."

Ella shook her head. "You were never my competition. These paintings deserve an audience focused on art. Shoppers in *Precious Things* are mostly browsing or impulse-buying. You don't impulse-buy one of these." She waved at Michael's paintings.

Her favorite painting had a red sticker. She squashed the momentary feeling of sadness and glanced around the room.

"Michael's spotted you," Alison said. "Here he comes."

Excitement radiated from the young artist who enveloped Ella in a hug. "Look at this! Isn't it wonderful?"

Ella beamed. "It's brilliant. Have you sold everything?"

"Not everything. There are still a couple of smaller ones to sell." He scanned her head to toe. "You're looking particularly fine tonight. I'm so glad you came."

"I wouldn't miss it." But she almost had—if it hadn't been for Louise, she would have stayed home emptying boxes on her own, rather than living life.

Michael pointed at the magnificent seascape that formed the display's centerpiece and had once had pride of place in *Precious Things*. "That's your favorite, isn't it?"

She nodded.

"See the red sticker?"

"I'm so glad. Some fortunate person will love hanging that on their wall."

Michael grinned. "I stickered it. You've done so much, believing in me and giving me wall space when I arrived at the shop with my paintings stuffed onto the backseat of my car. This painting is a present. From me to you."

It took Ella a few moments to recover enough to splutter out her thanks, then Michael was being hailed by another group of friends and supporters and took his leave. Ella looked at Alison. "You knew?"

"Of course. But it was his surprise to deliver. When's Amber home?"

"Should be in the next few days. We talk every week, and she's getting on great, but I've missed her." Every time she'd told Louise how she missed her only child, Louise immediately reminded her that Amber was having the experience of a lifetime, going to college in Dublin. Then followed up with how Ella's father must have missed her when she was Amber's age and had done the same thing. But Alison was more sensitive.

"It must be difficult. Especially with the divorce, and all."

"Everything changes, I guess. It isn't easy to give Amber stability now that the house is gone, and Jason and I live separate lives. Jason's new relationship is getting more serious. Amber's trying, but she told me she feels awkward around his girlfriend." She swapped her empty glass for a fresh glass of wine from a passing server. "Change is never easy, is it?"

"Change is necessary, though. There's no fighting it. And good things can come from change—just look at me." Alison opened her arms wide as if encouraging her friend to do precisely that. "Two years ago, I didn't think I'd survive. Now, I'm not only healthy but am doing what I've always wanted. If I hadn't had the health scare, I'd still be working a dead-end job I hate. It took the prospect of losing everything to make me go for what I want."

She hadn't talked to Louise since Jason's visit. She'd made time to get some legal advice, but their agreement at the time of the divorce seemed iron-clad. The prospect of losing the shop was burning her up, but she couldn't see an easy solution.

"I need to talk to Louise. Congratulations once again, the gallery is wonderful."

# Chapter Two

Ella grabbed a couple of glasses of sparkling wine from a passing waiter and headed for Louise. "Hey, you got a minute?"

"Sure." Louise eyed her carefully. "What's up?"

"We need to talk."

Louise's eyes widened. "Is this about Jason's visit?"

Louise had left *Precious Things* to collect stock while Ella was talking with Jason, and they hadn't yet had *the talk*. Ella had been quiet and reserved ever since Jason dropped his bombshell, not because she didn't want to share with her best friend, but because she was still processing.

Once again, a decision Jason made was blowing up her life.

The divorce had been a trial. Selling the family home and seeing their daughter head off to college in another country far away had been harder. Still, at least she'd always had the security of *Precious Things* and the daily routine of dealing with clients and customers and spending time with Louise. Now even that was at risk, just because Jason snapped his fingers and delivered an ultimatum.

"Yes."

"Here?" Louise looked around the crowded gallery, then spied a door leading into the pretty garden in the back. A space a realtor would describe as bijoux rather than cramped. "Or outside?"

"Outside."

She followed Louise through the browsers and bummed a cigarette from someone smoking just outside the door.

"You don't smoke." Louise frowned as Ella took a puff, coughed, and swallowed a mouthful of wine.

"I did once." Twenty years ago. She took another drag. "I thought it might help." Her head swam. "God knows why." She ground it out in an ashtray on a small wrought-iron table. "It doesn't."

"No. It wouldn't." Louise pulled out a chair and guided her onto it, then sat too. "What did he say to you? I've been worried sick."

There could be no way of sugar-coating it. "Jason wants to sell *Precious Things*."

Louise frowned. "But the business is yours. You have that in writing. And you inherited the premises in your grandmother's will; it's a family asset."

"He can't touch the company, but the premises is a different matter. He owns fifty percent, and he's given me three months to either buy out his half, or we'll have to sell and split the proceeds."

The futility of the situation, the creeping sense of horror at the prospect of losing the last thing she could call hers, was almost overwhelming.

"How much?"

"The shop is prime real estate. I don't know what it's worth, but it must be seven-hundred, maybe as high as eight-hundred thousand."

"Ouch." Louise swallowed her drink and abandoned her glass. "You know I'd buy in if I could afford it, I could raise a hundred grand, but half of seven is way beyond my budget."

"Beyond mine, too. I plowed my savings into renewing our stock and the refit last year. I don't have any ready funds, and of course, he knows that."

"What will you do?"

"I've tried the bank—they turned me down flat. I'm thinking of selling my house."

"You can't. You love that house."

"I know. It stinks."

Jason knew more than anyone how she needed to have somewhere to call her own. She needed the security of owning her home. She was risk-averse. Notoriously reticent to venture out of her comfort zone.

"Why does he have to do this?" Louise wailed, but they both knew the answer.

Ella answered anyway. "He needs money. I guess him owning half the building was always going to be a problem, but I hoped he'd just let it slide."

In retrospect, she'd been naive. Part of her had always known he'd sever the last remaining tie with their old life, but she'd opted to ignore that fact.

"There's always your mother?" Louise whispered. Her eyebrows rose, and her mouth twisted into a wry smile. She looked like a pixie trying to sell a complete wreck of a second-hand car.

"There is never my mother." One word in the right ear from her widowed mother, and a bank loan would be instantly forthcoming, but the cost—the cost was unpayable. Family should take sides in divorces—but not the way Eloise had. Despite her son-in-law's philandering, she'd come down firmly in his corner.

"He needs variety; he's a man!" had been her reaction to news of his cheating.

"You could have a little procedure. Dr. Sharp is fantastic." She pulled aside her scarf to show off her newly wrinkle-free neck. "Maybe get your boobs perked up while you're there? Gravity..." She'd shaken her head while gazing at her daughter's chest.

There was no way in hell she'd ask her mother for money.

"So, you find a business partner who will buy into the building as well as the business, or sell the shop and buy somewhere new. Somewhere smaller."

"Where, exactly? It's not as if there's anywhere for sale around here in my budget. And our clients buy from us because we're right on their doorsteps. If we move somewhere else, we'll have to start all over again and be in competition with a whole raft of other stores." Ella rubbed the back of her neck. "Our location is key to *Precious Things'* success. I can't lose it. People drive around the curve of the bay, and wham, there we are, inviting them to come inside and browse. Location is such a large part of the store's appeal. No, the only solution will be to sell the beach house and pay him off."

Her world had changed. For a long time, she'd plastered on a smile, not let the world see how she was falling apart behind her composed exterior. She hadn't thought there could be anything worse than that first blow—finding that Jason had been cheating. But there had.

Through it all, sitting outside her house, her tiny haven by the sea had been the only balm to soothe her soul. Alone with the sound of the sea for company, she could close her eyes and feel the heat of the sun on her face. Accept that she was battered and bruised but alive. That life had a purpose, and if she could only get through this horrible interlude, there was a brighter life awaiting her.

Now that future was in danger. Swirling uncertainty was retaking hold.

Without money to buy him out, the future of her business was in danger.

Without the beach house, she'd be homeless, but what other choice did she have?

* * *

Chris chose the venue—*Carpaccio Carpaccio*, an Italian restaurant on the bay peninsula that had been there forever.

Ella had never eaten there. Large windows faced the street, and inside, the restaurant was bright and airy, with open beams and reclaimed wood panels on the walls, which gave the place a warm, homespun vibe. The tables were waxed pine, functional rather than elegant, and the kitchen-type chairs were a mishmash of old and modern, painted and plain wood. It wasn't the sort of place she expected Chris to choose, but he'd assured her it had the best Italian food in the county.

Chris rose when he saw her walk in, and pulled out her chair in a show of old-fashioned courtesy. He'd dressed smart-casual: pale chinos and a cream linen jacket over a white shirt left open at the neck. He was immensely good-looking. If it weren't for his lime green converse sneakers, she could almost pretend she was lunching with George.

"Babe."

Until he opened his mouth.

"Please don't call me that, Chris." She forced a smile.

"I thought, seeing as we were becoming better friends...."

"Yeah, well, friends don't demean friends by calling them babe. Not in this day and age."

Chris's laugh was more a snort than anything else. "Honey, you need to take a chill pill."

"Honey is no better. I have a name. Just use that." Her tone was sharper than she intended, but god, who the hell said take a chill pill anymore?

"Ella—"

"That's better." God, she'd been acting like a total bitch. It wasn't his fault he was such an idiot. She smiled. "I'm sorry, it's just been a tough morning,"

Chris looked across the room, held up his hand, and clicked his fingers. A waiter scurried over carrying an ice bucket he placed on the edge of the table. Chilling inside was a bottle of prosecco.

"In that case, you'll be ready for a drink."

She'd already verbally slapped Chris down a couple of times since arriving. Refusing to drink alcohol over lunch when he'd taken the trouble to arrange it all beforehand seemed churlish. Where had the rules she'd lived by got her anyway? Was the world likely to end if she got pissed over lunch?

"Lovely."

The waiter filled her glass to the brim. She downed half of it in one.

"Steady on...we don't want that going to your head. Or do we?" He wiggled his eyebrows.

Ella laughed. "God, you're incorrigible."

Chris grinned. He flipped open his menu. "Let's order. I'm starving."

Why the hell should she not have a drink with lunch? Ella sipped her second glass of prosecco and toyed with her garlic mushrooms. Jason hated her eating anything with garlic. Said it made her smell awful. Nineteen years of denying herself the pleasure of garlic mushrooms. Nineteen years of catching up to do. "Fantastic."

"What?"

Ella blinked rapidly. Shit, did I say that out loud?

"I was thinking of the way you source your pashminas. Providing a market for artisan craftspeople. Fantastic." She scooped in another mouthful of mushrooms and moaned.

Chris's eyes widened. His ankle brushed against hers under the table.

She shifted her legs to the side, away from him. "I'm moaning because I haven't eaten garlic mushrooms for such a long time—I'd forgotten how much I enjoy them."

"They are good, aren't they?" The moment she'd chosen the appetizer, he followed suit. Presumably because if there were to be kissing later, it would make the co-mingling of tongues more pleasurable.

She twisted her head to one side, considering.

"Another glass?'

Fuck it. Live dangerously. "Go for it."

"You're different today. More relaxed." They demolished their appetizers, chatted over the mains, and dissected politics and movies over dessert. Ella hadn't eaten so much in one meal since she was a student—pizza loaded with cheese and a tiramisu to-die-for dessert, and as they sipped coffee, the booze buzz mingled with the sugar hit in an immensely pleasurable way.

"It's the drink."

Chris shook his head. "You were like that before you started drinking."

"I've had a lot going on recently. Personal stuff." The intimate restaurant felt like a safe space. Maybe all Chris wanted was to get into her bed, but wasn't everyone looking for a connection? Didn't everyone deserve happiness, no matter how fleeting?

"Your divorce."

She nodded. "The divorce, my daughter going away for college, other stuff...." He was one of their suppliers. She couldn't let him know about any business matters. "My whole life is completely different than it was a year ago. It takes some getting used to."

Chris leaned across the table and placed his hand on hers.

His gold chain bracelet slid forward and pressed against her skin. "I know it can. I've been divorced twice. But life goes on. It would help if you embraced change. I want to help you with the transition if you let me." His dark-chocolate eyes gleamed with what looked like sincerity. "The first step is sleeping with someone new."

Ella's hand twitched under his. She wanted to pull it away, but that would be too extreme a reaction to his words. And besides, he'd given her a good time. There was no need to spoil things by acting offended.

"I'm not ready for that yet." She carefully extricated her hand to pick up her coffee cup. "I've really enjoyed our lunch date. Thank you."

"Maybe next time we can make it dinner."

"I think maybe you're looking for something I'm not ready to give. We're in different places right now, I—"

Chris lifted his coffee cup, and something happened; she wasn't sure what, but then the cup upended, and the warm liquid soaked the front of his shirt, dripping onto the table.

"Shit!" He placed the cup on the table. "I'm so clumsy."

She passed him her napkin, and the waiter rushed over to help.

"That'll never come out." He looked down. His white shirt and pale linen jacket were tinged brown with cappuccino splashes.

"It'll be fine. You need to rinse it in cold water straight away, and if that doesn't work, pre-treat with detergent."

His look of incomprehension was a classic. "I have a woman who comes in a couple of days a week. She does stuff like laundry. She'll handle it on Thursday."

By Thursday, there'd be no hope in saving either the shirt or his jacket. "Ask for the check. There's a general store around the corner. I'm sure they'll have what we need."

There wasn't a stain in the world that wouldn't come out.

And being a domestic goddess was one of the little things she'd taken pride in, once upon a time. But did anyone really respect her encyclopaedic knowledge of the right solution to remove red wine from a carpet, blood from bedsheets, spilled coffee from a white rug?

No, they didn't.

Knowing how to clean translated into doing the cleaning. And Chris didn't even know if he had any laundry detergent, or if his housekeeper brought it with her. So, rather than go with her instinct to take over the task at hand, Ella pointed out detergent and pre-treatment products in the store, and made to leave.

Easier said than done. Her steps were unsteady. Exposure to the fresh air made the alcohol go straight to her head. At barely three-thirty in the afternoon, she could hardly work out the bus timetable, never mind catch the right bus.

She tripped on the way out of the store, and Chris caught her arm; steadied her.

"My apartment is just around the corner. Why don't you come back, and we'll grab another cup of coffee?"

"I should take a taxi."

"We can call one from the apartment."

She couldn't go home in this state—what if one of the neighbors spotted her—stopped, and wanted to chat? Her breath was a potent mix of prosecco and garlic, and her head was pounding. There were painkillers in her purse. She always carried painkillers, safety pins, and clear nail varnish in case of a snag in her hose, so going to Chris's apartment seemed the sensible solution.

That crazy thought she had earlier, of kissing him, had receded into the background, and it seemed to have for him, too. Coffee. Sober up. Taxi home. It all sounded like a good plan.

"Home sweet home." Chris swung the door open wide,

and she stepped straight from the outside into his living room in one step. It was one of the smallest apartments she'd ever visited.

"Let me show you around." Chris took a couple of steps to the right and patted a slim countertop. "The kitchen area." He flipped down a table fastened into a cupboard on the wall. "Dining room." He waved a hand at the love seat facing the TV. "Sitting room, which doubles as a bedroom." Chris opened a door to the left. "Bathroom."

Ella glanced around. No garden. No place to dry clothes, and no sign of a washing machine, even.

"So when you say that your housekeeper does the laundry, I'm guessing she takes it away with her?"

"She does." Chris flipped up the couch seat, pulled out a sofabed, and reached under it to retrieve a plastic box from which he recovered a Walking Dead tee-shirt. He took off his jacket and stripped off his shirt. "There's a Keurig on the counter. Make us a couple of coffees, will you?"

"Give me that shirt."

He tossed it over, and Ella caught it in mid-air. She looked at the sink full of dishes.

"I'll just...." She grabbed the detergent, opened the door to the tiny bathroom, and poured cold water into the sink.

"I used to have a bigger place—but two sets of alimony...."

His voice drifted in from the next room as she swirled detergent into the water and dunked his shirt. She'd thought her beach house was small, but this place was tiny. There was just enough room to hang the shirt over the showerhead but not enough room to deal with the jacket. And once again, instead of having a grown-up lunch with a guy, she was relegated to laundry. By her choice. If she kept at it, he'd doubtless hand over underwear and socks for her to wash, too.

She pushed the shirt down in the water.

Dried her hands.

Called a cab.

Damn the coffee. Life had sobered her right up.

"I have to leave." She stepped back into the room that was Chris's everything. He held the tee-shirt in his hands, bare-chested, and tried what must be his most winning smile.

"You should stay."

"You'll need to take your jacket to the cleaners. You won't be able to process it properly here. Get it to them today, before it dries, and tell them what you spilled on it."

Chris walked forward and reached for her face. "Kiss me, babe."

She opened her mouth to tell him not to call her babe. Unfortunately, he took that as an invitation to lean in and plant a wet kiss on her mouth.

Her mouth clamped shut like a clamshell, changing the kiss from smooch to smoosh.

She stepped back. Then the tune "Pocket Full of Sunshine" blared through the silence. Saved by the ringtone.

"I have to get that. It's my daughter."

"Honey, babe..." Chris's hands found her hips. Forget politeness. If her subtle messages weren't getting across, she'd have to go for obvious.

"I'm not your honey, and I'm not your babe, or your baby, or sweetie, or any of the other stupid little names you like to call women."

She retrieved her phone, but too late. The ringing had stopped. *Damn.*

"I have to call my daughter back, and the cab will be picking me up outside in a couple of minutes." She scooped up her jacket from the chair. "Thanks for lunch, but as I said, I'm not looking for a relationship—"

"Who said anything about a relationship? I thought I could break your dry spell, that's all. Give us both some mutually assured satisfaction." He tried the eyebrow wiggle again, but it was too late. That particular ploy had lost its appeal forever.

"I don't want sex. I'm sorry if you got the wrong idea, but that's your problem, not mine."

Chris looked like a puppy that had been thoroughly kicked.

"Let the shirt soak for ten minutes, then rinse it and hang it over your showerhead." She reached for the door handle and let herself out.

# Chapter Three

*In a cab. Will call in ten.*

Ella texted her daughter and leaned back in the cab, breathing deeply. She had almost made a huge mistake due to her distress about Jason and the impossible position he'd put her in, sleepwalking into something she neither needed nor wanted. Just because other people told her it was time she jumped back into the sea in hopes of catching one of those 'plenty more fish' didn't mean she had to believe them.

She had made a colossal mistake once, which had changed her life's trajectory. She wouldn't do it again.

Why couldn't she be happy with what she was? There were more exciting things to do in life than tie yourself to a man, no matter how handsome. Men—even one-night stand men—were too much work.

Amber would be home before she knew it. She must be ringing with flight details.

The thought of the two of them spending a long, hot summer together made Ella smile.

"Take the next left. The traffic's light this time of day."

The cabbie met her gaze in the rearview mirror and nodded.

"Pocket Full of Sunshine" rang out as she was kicking off her shoes and settling on the couch. A warm feeling settled in Ella's chest. Her daughter was so keen to talk she couldn't even wait for her mom to call back.

"Hi, Mom!"

"Hi, Darling, how's it going?" So many questions to ask since their last phone call two weeks ago. So many new experiences her baby must be having. It was challenging to keep from switching into what Amber called 'interrormom' mode. Ella'd found the term funny when Jason coined it but now hated it. The word interrogating had rabid overtones, didn't it? When all she was doing was being interested. Connecting. Being everything a parent should be.

"Sorry to have missed your last call. I've been having such a great time." Amber was bubbly to the max, and her enthusiasm bled through the miles between them.

"Classes good? Are you keeping up with the course load?"

"Yeah, yeah." Amber sounded impatient. "But that's not why I'm calling. I know you're expecting me back for the summer, but...."

Ella's stomach rumbled. Maybe those garlic mushrooms—maybe a portent of what was to come.

"I've changed my plans. I'm going to a Greek island instead!"

Ella picked at a strand of loose wool fringing on the handwoven Mexican throw covering the sofa. Shoddy workmanship. She'd need to check the rest of the stock back at *Precious Things*; hopefully, this was a one-off, and the others were of better quality.

"Mom, did you hear me?" Uncertainty had crept into Amber's voice.

"I heard you. But I don't understand what you mean. I thought you were coming home for the summer. I put the money for your ticket home into your bank account a month ago; I thought you'd already bought your ticket."

"I was coming home, but Liam and I—"

"Liam?"

"I told you about him, remember? We've been dating since January. Anyway, he's studying ancient history and had arranged to go on a dig this summer on this amazing little island off Greece called Kosmima. I'm going with him."

"You're not coming home? At all?" Ella mentally cursed at the break in her voice, but the disappointment was more than she could take. There was silence down the other end of the phone. Amber must be wondering what to say. How to smooth things over with her ancient, needy mother.

Ella took a deep breath. She scrunched up her eyes tight. "So this thing with Liam is serious?"

Amber. Cute, fun-loving Amber had never been serious about a boy before.

"Very serious, Mom. That's why else I'm calling. Liam asked me to marry him. And I said yes!"

Ella wanted to shout or to scream. She bit back the question she burned to ask. Surely Amber knew there was no need to marry the guy, even if there was a baby on the way? Jesus.

Ella spoke again. "And before you ask, no, I'm not pregnant."

She must proceed cautiously. If Ella said the wrong thing now, she'd alienate Amber forever. *Stall. Stall.* "Your father—"

"Liam asked Dad for my hand over Skype last night. Isn't that romantic? And of course, Dad said yes and gave us his blessing."

Of course he did.

"So Dad knows all about this."

"He and Betsy are happy for us." Amber's tone was defiant.

"I-I… I'd love to meet Liam. How old is he?"

"He's the same age as me, eighteen."

"You're both very young to be thinking of getting married." Ella tried to infuse understanding and warmth into her voice. "Surely, there's no need to rush into anything, especially if you're not pregnant."

"We want to be together, Mom. He's wonderful. When you meet the one you want to spend your life with, you know, don't you? You know it in every fiber of your body. You don't want to let that one get away."

"What about Liam's parents? Have you told them?"

Ella needed an ally. Someone to persuade them both that tying themselves to another forever while still in their teens was a crazy idea that held more risks than advantages.

"Liam's mother is dead. He wants to tell his father face-to-face. That's why we're going to Kosmima. His dad is the archaeologist running the dig." Amber paused for breath. "I know you think we're too young, and Liam's worried his father will think so too. But once he meets me—once he sees how perfect we are for each other. Liam's sure he'll be on board with our getting married. I want you to be happy for me, Mom. With Liam by my side, I feel like I can rule the whole world. Like there's nothing I can't do."

There was no way in hell Amber was getting hitched at eighteen. No way in hell.

"When are you planning the ceremony?" Maybe they could have a long engagement. Anything could happen in a couple of years. If they were still together after that amount of time passed…

"We want to get married over the Christmas vacation. In Monterey. Just family and a few friends. Being home would make it so special. And I need to talk to you and Dad about next year; I don't know if I want to continue with my course or whether it would be a better idea to—"

Ella anticipated what Amber might say but couldn't bear to hear it. "Okay, honey. You've given me quite a lot to think about. I'm glad that you're happy." Ella wasn't happy about the wedding, but there was nothing she could do about it without being face to face with her daughter. And if Amber wanted to drop out of college, that sure wasn't a discussion she would be having over the telephone.

"Your phone bill will be blowing up. Let's talk again soon."

Ella hung up, then lay facedown on the sofa. And groaned.

* * *

Ella was at her desk considering her options when Louise walked into *Precious Things* the following morning. Louise took one look at the papers scattered haphazardly over the surface and walked straight across the room.

"You look busy. Trying to work out a save-the-shop scenario?"

"Things have progressed since Jason." She swiveled to snatch a page from the printer. "There's a new problem."

Louise's eyes widened. She handed over the take-out cup of coffee and sat. "Tell me."

"Amber's not coming home. She's running away to some island with a boy."

Louise shrugged. "I know you're dying to see her, but romance—you know how these things go—she's young, she probably just wants an adventure."

"She wants more than that. She wants marriage."

"What?" Louise's mouth dropped open. The look of shock written all over her face showed she fully understood the severity of the situation. "She can't get married. She's barely out of diapers!"

"Tell me about it." Ella puffed out a breath. "She's not pregnant, thank god, but she's persuaded herself that she should follow her heart and accept this boy's proposal. He's the same age. I don't know what kids think they're doing these days." When she was a little older than Amber, Jason had proposed, to Ella's mother's delight. She'd urged her daughter to accept his proposal quickly before he changed his mind. Had emphasized how lucky she was to have found a man who wanted to marry her, especially after the *disgraceful incident*.

Things had sure changed. Now, the thought of Amber settling down with one man forever at such a young age sent Ella into full-on panic mode.

"That's outrageous. You can't let Amber do it. I know you don't want to have anything to do with Jason at the moment, but maybe if the two of you formed a united front—"

"Too late for that. Liam asked Jason for her hand, and he gave them his blessing."

"That man...." Louise's eyes flashed. "He really is a total prick."

"Tell me about it."

"So, Liam. That's the boy?"

"Yes. He's Irish. It was bad enough knowing I'd lose Amber for four years studying in Trinity College, but if she gets married, she'll never come home. And even more worrying, I think she's considering dropping out of college." Despair flooded her. Could she bear living on the other side of the world from her only child? And what if Amber had kids eventually? Would she have anything in common with her grandchildren? Would she even be able to afford to visit more than once a year? A year is a long time in a child's life.

"So, what's the plan?"

Ella flipped the top off her coffee and discarded it on the desk. A drip smeared the surface, but she paid it no heed—there were more pressing problems than untidiness today. She picked up the page she'd just printed and handed it to her friend.

"I thought the first thing would be to track him down on Facebook. See what I could learn about him." She frowned. "But that's easier said than done. Amber's Facebook is locked down tighter than a brothel at Easter. I tried to be considerate and not to invade her online privacy, so I never asked to be friends on Facebook—god, I'm regretting that now."

"I'm friends with her. Calm down. I'll log in." Louise flipped open her laptop and started the process.

Ella rounded the desk and peered over her friend's shoulder.

"She hasn't put any pictures up of them together," she said after a quick scan. "And she hasn't broadcast her relationship status either."

Damn, damn, damn. Amber had taken those lessons about being discreet on social media to heart. For once, Ella wished she hadn't been such a vigilant parent.

"I'll check her friend list." Louise leaned close to the screen and scrolled. Fresh-faced teens flew past rapidly. "Here's a Liam." She kept scrolling. "Ah. Here's another. And another."

Three bloody Liams in Amber's friend list. Why hadn't she paid more attention when her daughter told her about her new boyfriend? She couldn't remember any pertinent details—not even his hair color.

"Which one is it?" Louise looked up. "What's his full name?"

"I don't know." Despair took hold and squeezed her guts. "Let's have a look at them and see if we can work it out."

"Liam number one likes Kylie, cocktails, and karaoke."

"You sound like the host of a dating show."

Louise grinned. "Liam number two seems to favor craft beer and heavy metal." She clicked through to his profile and scanned his pictures. "He also seems to like going out with all his friends and getting shitfaced." She played a snippet of rowdy video. "I'm guessing Liam number two isn't our boy."

She flicked back to the friends' list. "Liam number three likes sailing and rugby." She raised an eyebrow. "And he's definitely the hottest of the bunch." She waved at a picture. "Amber's type, do you think?"

From feeling as though she knew everything about her daughter's life, Ella realized she knew next to nothing. Not even Amber's type.

"Any hints on his page? Photos?"

Louise tapped on the keyboard. Scrolled on the trackpad. "No details. He could work for the CIA."

"I've logged a friend request. Once she approves me, I'll go through it all forensically at home. Is Amber on any other social media that you know of?"

The question was humiliating. Surely Ella should know more about Amber's digital footprint.

"Just Instagram, I think."

"If I can get a ticket, I could fly over to Dublin before they leave for Kosmima. I could take them out to dinner. Talk some sense into them."

Louise's nose wrinkled. "That's hardly likely to work."

Her friend was right. If Liam had given her a ring, Ella wouldn't talk them out of their plans over a dinner date. She rubbed the ache at her temples.

"What about the shop? What about Jason trying to take it over?"

There were so many things to worry about. So many concerns demanded attention. Ella felt ripped in two with the pressure of all her responsibilities bearing down on her. But at the end of the day, only one thing mattered. Amber. She could live with losing the shop, but she couldn't live with not being there for her daughter when she needed her.

"I'll talk to him today. See if I can put a hold on everything until I've had a chance to sort this situation with Amber."

Louise checked her email. "A bride emailed to say she wants to order eight of the peach pashminas as wraps for her bridesmaids. We'll have to put in another order to Chris." She shot a flirty side-eye in Ella's direction. "Do you want to call him, or will I?"

"Uh. That date."

"Not good?"

Ella shoved the pages in front of her to one side. "Disastrous. I've been working on sorting out all of this for hours. I need a break. Let me tell you all about how I drank way too much prosecco and ended doing his fucking laundry."

* * *

Ella met Jason at the Starbucks around the corner from his office. In all the years they'd been married, he'd never met her here for coffee—he rarely met her anywhere but at the home they shared. He'd warned he could only spare five minutes and glanced at his watch the moment he strode through the door.

Jason picked up a regular americano in a take-out cup and joined her at a table near the door.

"I don't have long."

"You said."

"If you want to argue about the shop, you really should go through my lawyer."

"I don't want to argue about the shop. I want to talk about our daughter. She called last night to tell me her news."

Jason's mood shifted. He sipped his drink as though he didn't have a care in the world. As if he could think of nothing better than Amber becoming a Mrs. Mrs. who? It struck Ella that she didn't even know Liam's surname.

"It's great."

"Do you seriously think so?" Who was this man that she married? Could he seriously not see the downside to this scenario? "Amber's so young; she can't possibly know what she wants."

"We were young. We knew what we wanted." The way he looked at her—with echoes of the man she once loved in his eyes—softened her heart. "We wanted each other."

"Until one of us wanted someone else." The pain of his betrayal lanced her anew. "But that's not why we're here. I don't want to rehash what happened between us, Jason. I want to talk about our daughter. I think she's too young to make this decision. She's away from home in a new country, and she's vulnerable. She's trying new things, reveling in her newfound freedom—"

"Like mother, like daughter?"

"You would have to bring that up, wouldn't you?" Everything was always her fault. When Amber excelled in school, he called her 'our daughter', but her parentage was firmly attributed to Ella alone any time she was demanding. This time, however, the parallels were too obvious to deny. "I guess you have a point. When I left home and went to Ireland to study, I couldn't wait to try new things. I did, and I screwed up."

"The *disgraceful incident.*"

"Yes. As my mother labeled it: the *disgraceful incident*. I'm not proud of what I did. I've never been proud of it."

"Your parents dealt with your transgression by playing the

parent card. Do you think bullying Amber—forcing her to do your will at the expense of her happiness is the way to go? Because it sounds a lot to me like history repeating."

He always had the ability to hurt.

"You gave them your blessing." She couldn't keep the sting out of her voice.

"Amber rang me in the middle of the night and put her boyfriend on the phone. The guy was so nervous his voice shook. But when he spoke about Amber, he was sincere and passionate. He told me how much he loves her. How they can't bear to be apart, and how his life is complete with her by his side. Then he asked for my permission to propose. She must have been sitting right next to him because I heard her murmuring in the background. I couldn't break her heart by saying no. I don't know why you have it in for the boy. He sounds great."

"I've never spoken to him. I don't know what he looks like. I don't even know his full name."

"It's Dempsey. Liam Dempsey. Betsy's friended him on Facebook. Good-looking guy."

Dempsey. Liam number three. Dark hair, bright blue eyes, the most handsome Liam of the three. What had his profile said: he liked sailing?

"I can't believe you gave him your blessing without even talking to me about it." Her head pounded, and it wasn't just from the overload of coffee.

"It was two o'clock in the morning. Betsy was giving me the evil eye because I disturbed her beauty sleep. I had to take the call downstairs to the kitchen. I was on the phone, but even if I'd called you on the landline, I doubt you'd have taken a call from me in the middle of the night, would you?"

She wouldn't, Ella reluctantly conceded with a half-nod, half-shrug.

"Look, if she loves him, it'll all work out. And if they fall out of love, I'll make damn sure there's an iron-clad pre-nup."

"Did she say anything to you about not staying in college? Because if she did, that's a serious problem. Her future would be in jeopardy. She's such a good scholar with so much potential."

"She's studying computer science. She could do that anywhere, and she has so much raw talent, I'm sure she could talk her way into any company, with or without a degree." He took another sip of coffee. "I think, Ella, you'll have to accept that you don't have control over her anymore. Amber will do what she wants. And she's eighteen, not eight. If she decides to quit college and take her life in another direction, I, for one, will support her."

His righteous, 'I'm the most sympathetic parent' pitch—especially in light of the way he'd callously broken apart their family with no consideration of how that might affect their child whatsoever—left Ella speechless.

"Oh, and while we're talking, Betsy wanted me to ask you, you know that Rolodex of names and addresses you use for the Christmas cards? Can she have it? We need it."

Ella breathed in deep and ignored his question. She could say one thing about Jason. He had always cared about Amber. He may have ended up being a terrible husband, but he had been a good father.

"I want to make sure she's okay."

"I know you do."

"I can't concentrate on Amber if I'm battling with you about *Precious Things.* "I want to talk to Amber. I want to see her and meet this boy who wants to marry her. And I also want to make damn sure she doesn't do anything stupid. I want to assure myself that she's okay."

"But she's not coming home this summer."

"I want a temporary cease-fire. I need an extra month."

"I can't give it to you; I'm sorry. Three months is the best I can do. And if by any chance she decides she doesn't want to study in Ireland any longer, is there any chance of breaking the education fund and splitting it?"

Leopards never change their spots.

# Chapter Four

Sandy, Ella's realtor, couldn't believe her luck. At least, that was Ella's reading of the other woman's mental state as they stood in Ella's living room.

"You've done wonders with the place." Sandy fingered the throw on the new couch. "It looked good before—" She glanced out at the ocean from the huge picture window—"but now, you've taken it up to the next level."

She blew out a breath, then shook her head as a smile softened the harsh line of her mouth. "And that view, am I right? All waterside property in California holds its value, and even in the short amount of time you've owned the cottage, prices have inched up a little. But the improvements—the money you've poured in to upgrade the kitchen have added another ten grand straight away."

She fished in her purse, extracted her phone, opened a calculator, and started tapping.

"Are you sure you want to sell?" She glanced up over the rim of her sunglasses. "I shouldn't look a gift horse in the mouth, but you love this house. I know you do."

"I do love it." Pain blossomed in the center of Ella's chest.

As though someone tied a rope around her heart and tugged. "It's the first place I've bought that's all mine. But things have changed, and I need to evaluate all of my options." She slid open the glass door that led out onto the deck. "Come see what I did with the garden, and then we'll drive on up to *Precious Things*."

Louise was delivering a pair of gilt chairs with tapestry seats to one of their clients an hour away. Ella hated bringing Sandy to the store while her friend was out—it felt disloyal somehow. She was the sole owner of the premises; Louise had never wanted to buy in to the business, but they spent every day working together, and *Precious Things* always felt like it belonged to both of them.

When it came right down to it, though, it didn't. Ella was the only person responsible for paying the bills—the only person who needed to sort out this whole mess.

She drove up to the front door and looked away to hide her grimace as Sandy bounced out of the car and started taking pictures. "I've wanted to have a property on this road forever," she breathed. "And this place is spectacular. How many square feet?"

"I don't exactly know. We'll have to measure." The urge to bundle the realtor back into the car and speed away was strong, but she resisted the impulse. "You know, at this stage, I'm not certain about selling the premises; I just want to investigate my options."

"You said." Sandy stood at the front door, hands cupping the glass to cut down on glare as she peered into the interior. "Can I see inside?"

Sandy was ready for anything. She extracted a digital measuring tape from her purse, taking measurements and tapping them into her calculator app with ease. "There's a room back here?"

Ella nodded, but Sandy hadn't even waited for a response.

She was tracking into the back office with zeal, leaving Ella trailing in her wake. Memories assailed her as Sandy opened the back door to check the tiny yard.

When she was a small child, and this was her grandfather's store, she'd visited with her mother.

He'd started his jewelry business here in the 1950s, and this building was where his company had grown. By the time his son was married, he had a fleet of stores, but he still held on to his flagship. He'd left it to his wife, who willed it to her only granddaughter. Selling felt like eradicating another part of her history. Worse, her family's history.

Opening *Precious Things* had been her attempt at stepping out of her husband's shadow. But despite her efforts, it had never been as fabulous as she hoped. The shop did moderate business—affording her and Louise a reasonable income, but no more than that.

Coffee and talk filled her days, with most of their business coming from selling overpriced sofas, tables, and chairs to the locals who found the appeal of *Precious Things* irresistible.

Her clientele were people who wanted the prettiest well-made items and were willing to pay for them. She'd built the business supplying items crafted by local artisans but hadn't worked to grow the business beyond picking up passing trade.

All of which was fine when she owned the building and didn't have to worry about rent, but now things were different.

"You could make a good income renting out the shop if you don't want to sell." Sandy pushed up her sunglasses and fixed Ella with a determined stare. "It's none of my business, but you seem as though you're going through something challenging here. Want to talk about it?"

"Divorce." The word should have been enough, but Sandy just nodded and waited for more. "My ex-husband owns half the building, and he wants his half."

Sandy sucked her teeth. "Oh, I see where you're coming from. That's rough."

"It's all pretty new. Jason told me this week that he needs us to sell."

"So you're evaluating everything."

"Yes. The best thing would be to buy him out. But that takes cash...." She shrugged. She turned the key in the back door then headed into the front of the shop.

"And that's where I come into the picture." Sandy flicked her shades back over her eyes. "Okay, I'll work those numbers and get in touch. Stay strong. You'll get through this."

* * *

Louise trekked across the sand barefoot to the bonfire Ella had built on the beach, carrying a large pizza box and two glasses, gripping a bottle of red wine under her arm.

Ella stood and relieved her of the glasses and wine. Louise sank onto the blanket. The warmth of the day had begun to fade, but the sand and rocks were still warm with banked heat. This area of the beach had a designated bonfire area—a stone circle which could be used by anyone. A breeze lifted a tendril of Ella's hair, and bounced it across her face. The salty sea scent overlaid with woodsmoke drifted in the air.

They poured wine and ate pizza, staring into the flickering flames.

"This is pleasant. Just felt like a change of scene?"

"Sort of." Ella savored a mouthful of the dark, fruity wine. She reached to her left and picked a few index cards from the stack resting in a Tupperware lunchbox. "I don't even know some of these people." She read the names, tossed one to the side, and threw the rest on the fire. "I've been sending Christmas cards to Jason's colleagues for years, and for all I know, some of them may be dead." She waved the card she'd discarded at Louise. "And this one? George and Alma Burnside? I've only saved them from the pyre because they send us —used to send us—a card every year. I have no idea who the hell they are. I think George worked with Jason sometimes. The only time they were ever mentioned was when the card came in every year. Jason would hold it up and say 'George and Alma' with a satisfied smile."

"You're saving the address details of someone you've never met because they send you a Christmas card every year?" Louise's brow wrinkled.

"Messed up, isn't it? And they won't send me one this year because I'm no longer Jason's wife." She threw the card into the fire. "He couldn't even be bothered to remember half these people, so why should I?"

"You were writing them all Christmas cards a few days ago."

"A lot can happen in a few days." She pointed at a pile of black, curled ash at the edge of the fire. "I wrote almost a hundred cards. I guess I didn't want them to think I'd been beaten by the divorce—that I no longer mattered. I was trying to maintain some twisted status quo. This evening, I went through them again, took out any I actually wanted to send to people I actually know, and torched the others. Do you know how many I kept?"

Her voice was high with a hysterical edge. She poured herself another glass of wine and drank to stop herself from repeating the question.

"How many?"

"Three."

Louise grimaced. "I'm sort of sad to see the old Rolodex go. It was a classic."

"She wanted it, you know. Betsy. I guess she thought she'd replaced me in every way that matters; why not take control of the Rolodex, too? I spent years writing details from the top of letters, and backs of envelopes. I took pride in compiling the Rolodex. Isn't that pathetic? Now Betsy wants it. Guess what —she can compile her own stuffing Christmas card list."

"She'll probably email a virtual card. That's what I'd do."

"I don't think emailing wedding invitations is the done thing, though. And I guess Jason wants to make sure he doesn't offend someone important by forgetting them."

"She asked for the Rolodex so she could send wedding invitations?"

"That's what I'm thinking. I don't know for sure. But Jason had that self-satisfied smirk in his voice. I heard it." She reached for another handful of cards and tossed them into the flames. "Bugger it. I can't even be bothered to read through the cards anymore. I want the whole lot burned."

Fragments of scorched paper danced in the air, propelled skyward by the heat of the fire. The beach was empty. The sand pristine. The setting sun painted the clouds every shade from pale apricot to cinnabar.

They ate pizza in a silence broken only by the whisper of the waves, the crackle of the burning logs. The scent of woodsmoke drifted in the air.

Louise shifted closer on the blanket and draped an arm over Ella's shoulders.

The fire had burned down to embers, and the colors in the sky had shifted to bruised purple and charcoal grey when Ella spoke again. "I've booked a flight."

Louise poked at the embers with a stick then shoved the empty pizza box onto the bonfire. Flames blazed bright orange as the fire consumed the oily cardboard. "To Dublin?"

"To Greece. I tried to sign on as a volunteer at the dig as a cover, but there are no more places available, so I'm just going out there anyway. Maybe I can change their minds."

She worried her bottom lip with her teeth as nerves gripped and twisted in her gut. There was little about the island online. The archeological site was mentioned in a stuffy journal, but there were no photographs or details about the place—just a list of the finds dug up over the past few years.

The Wikipedia entry was three lines. Size of the island: twenty-eight square miles split between one large town and two smaller settlements. The population seemed to be in the hundreds rather than thousands. There was a link to an academic journal entry about the archaeological dig—which was where she'd found the contact information to apply as a volunteer—as that was it.

She didn't even know if she could find a hotel on the island. But there must be somewhere she could stay. She'd find out more when she got there.

"You don't know anything about archaeology."

"My degree was in history of art and architecture."

"A degree you abandoned."

Ella nodded. "True. Although I didn't exactly abandon it, as you very well know, I was forced to quit after the *disgraceful incident*. I don't think I can take much more, Lou. I feel like I'm holding on to my sanity with my fingertips, and my grip is loosening. I need to take action—to take back control of my destiny. I know I'd booked a couple of weeks off for when Amber came home, but I might need you to hold down the fort for longer."

"Take as long as you need."

"You don't need to keep the shop open every day. Business is quiet at the moment. You can close up if you want to. Hang a 'gone fishing' sign on the door or something. I asked Jason for an extra month so I could spend time with Amber without worrying about the future, but he refused."

It was getting cold. Louise pulled the sides of her cardigan closed. "I'll open the shop every morning and do the basics. Might well take you up on your offer and close it by lunchtime every day if not much is going on."

Ella nodded. She picked up the bottle and dowsed the dying fire. "I've always been interested in art and culture. You know that. I always regretted never getting as far as Greece when I lived in Europe. This can be my chance. Instead of spending a couple of days with Amber in Dublin, I'll meet her on the island and try to talk her around."

"Does she know you're coming?"

Ella shook her head. "I don't want to give her an opportunity to tell me not to come. I leave Thursday."

# Chapter Five

Work was done for the day. The sun was low in the sky, and the camp was quiet for the first time in hours. Aidan Dempsey stared out over the scrubland, breathing in the aromatic scent of the rosemary and oregano plants that grew wild on the mountain. He'd worked on Kosmima for the past five summers and found it as fascinating now as he had that very first year. The tiny island didn't have the pulling power of its Greek island neighbors. There was only one hotel, and little in the way of restaurants. There were no cinemas—no theatre. And as a result, few tourists except for the student volunteers who signed up for the dig every summer.

But there was magic on this remote island. Magic he rarely saw in Dublin. The magic of nature. Keening sea birds swooped and dived from the clifftops. The sequin sparkle of the ocean when the sunshine played across its surface.

Over the years, he'd visited all of the villages on the island and had explored every inch of the coastline. Everywhere he went he was always greeted warmly, sometimes by friends, sometimes by people he didn't know.

The inhabitants of Kosmima extended the hand of friendship to strangers, and he felt happier here than he did the rest of the year in Dublin.

The volunteers weren't a rowdy crew, but there was always noise when twenty or thirty people got together. The sound of shovels scraping the arid soil. Chisels carefully tapping caked mud to release trapped artifacts. Even the murmur of voices as people shared their discoveries.

He stretched his elbows out to the side, and flexed his back. Being bent over all day played havoc with his muscles. It had been a hour since the team logged their finds and set off down the mountain toward the tiny town nestled out of sight in the foothills. Aidan's stomach grumbled. He must secure the site and join them before the light was gone—the last thing he needed was a twisted ankle from scrabbling over rocks in the dark. He headed into the tiny cabin next to the large canvas tent where the team processed the day's finds. There were a few more items to check, and then he was officially off duty.

A clearing of a throat announced he was no longer alone. "Someone is waiting for you at the cafe."

Probably one of the volunteers crying off for the morning. They'd worked harder today than many of them had probably been expecting. A hot bath was calling to Aidan, the last thing he wanted to do was spend more time chatting at the café.

Nick Balaska propped a shoulder against the frame of the doorway leading into the cabin. Two bottles of beer dangled from his fingers. "A woman."

*That's unexpected.* "A woman, huh? Which one?" Aidan Dempsey checked the Ziploc seal on a baggie containing a piece of pottery they'd excavated that morning, and made sure the volunteer had written the corresponding reference in the daybook correctly. He placed it into the large plastic box containing today's finds and snapped the box top shut.

"A stranger." Nick strolled in and slung his leg over the nearest chair, sitting with the chair back between his spread thighs. "Here." He handed Aidan a bottle. Then he rested his arm across the chair back and took a long swallow of beer. "An American."

"American?" There weren't any American volunteers this year. The foundation offered places to local students first and then to students from other European degree courses. They filled up quickly, and there was a waiting list. Liam and his girlfriend managed to secure places by applying early, but they had to turn around thirty people away—a record number. He rubbed a hand across the frown furrowing his brow. An American. He didn't even know any Americans. The only American woman he could think of was Liam's new girlfriend, but surely she and his son were traveling together. "Hold old is she?"

Nick grinned. "Late thirties?"

"So it's not the one I was thinking then."

Nick's eyebrows rose.

"I'm expecting Liam and his girlfriend. He said they were flying in at the weekend. She's his age, though."

Nick drained his beer. Rolled his shoulders. He and Aidan were the same height—six-four, but where Aidan had the rangy build of a runner, Nick was solid muscle, honed by countless hours working out. They'd met five years ago when Aidan assumed the position as team leader for the Kosmima excavation project. Nick was more than capable of heading the project but preferred to take the number two role to avoid dealing with the paperwork and all the admin bullshit that came as part and parcel of the job. The money between the two positions was minimal. Maybe Nick had got the better deal—considering. But dealing with the pencil pushers was a small price to pay for the pure, unadulterated joy of spending four glorious months on Kosmima every summer.

"I can't wait to see him. I missed him last year."

"Yeah, me, too." Once Liam finished school, he'd headed off on a tour of Europe with his school friends. Aidan couldn't blame him. He'd worked so hard on his exams and needed to blow off some steam before the results came out, and he discovered if he'd been successful in getting into the course he wanted in Trinity.

It had been a bittersweet wrench last year. Liam had eventually cast off his childish ways and become an adult. He was no longer a kid, and was ready to step out into the world, a grown man, one that liked, but didn't need, his father's support. Five years ago, the mere thought that Liam would grow into the man he was today was unthinkable. Day to day was all either of them could manage, putting one foot in front of the other, getting through one day, one week, one month, one year, a miracle that didn't seem achievable until it was.

Time was like that. Relentless.

Now the ache every time he thought of Carol was a dull one rather than a breath-stealing stabbing in his chest.

He finished checking the boxes. Made sure everything was secure. Chucked his empty beer bottle in the recycle box outside the shack's back door. Locked up. "So, what time are we meeting Kitten and her friend tonight?"

"Eleven."

Nick had been a good and loyal friend to Katerina 'Kitten' Gataki through the years of her disastrous marriage and after. He'd held off on asking her out, not wanting to put her under pressure or threaten their friendship, but the look in his eyes whenever they were together, the way he listened whenever she spoke, made his devotion to her obvious. At least to Aidan.

A month ago, Nick finally grew a pair and asked her on a date. Kitten had been waiting for him to make his move since she first met him. Their relationship had gone from zero to sixty in mere days. They were happy. And in the way of the newly love-stricken, Kitten seemed determined to spread the happiness by fixing up one of her single friends with Aidan.

In previous years, romance with anyone on the island hadn't been an issue. As a single father who spent half the year in Ireland, he wasn't anyone's idea of a long-term prospect, and there was no way he was leaving Liam alone at night—much as Liam might want him to. After five years, he knew most of the island's inhabitants. Having a quick fling with someone wouldn't go down well, and there was no way he was interested in any more than that with anyone.

"What's her friend's name again?"

"Sophia. She's the new chef at Twin Pines." The best, and only, hotel on the island.

"So Kitten's her boss."

"She didn't have to have her arm twisted, if that's what you're worried about. Kitten suggested a blind date, and Sophia was all for it."

"I don't know that this is such a good idea." Was there any way he could get out of going? The thought of disappointing a stranger's expectations made him come out in a sweat. He wasn't looking for a date. He didn't want to be set up. Had only agreed because Nick had been so determined, he didn't see how he could refuse.

"You like women, right?" Nick shot him a glance. "She's a woman. You haven't hooked up with anyone on the island for what, two years? I understand you not wanting your son to think you're a man-whore, but damn, Aidan, you don't have to live like a monk."

"I haven't been. Dating in a big city is easier, though. More discreet." They set off down the mountain toward town.

"So, who do you see in Dublin? Anyone serious?"

Three Tinder hookups with three different women in the past year. A few sleepovers at his friends with benefits' house.

Two lonely people, neither interested in any more than a few drinks and a quick roll between the sheets.

"No one. There's no one. I don't need anyone. I'm happy."

* * *

*Anything that can go wrong will go wrong.*

Ella heard her mother's voice in her head as she sipped her second glass of Retsina. Before the divorce, she'd been smug about her perfect life and had been frankly callous, spouting off about the power of attraction.

It was cringeworthy how she'd lectured heartbroken friends advising them to change their mindset to change their lives.

Since Jason, she'd learned the folly of that way of thinking.

But breaking old habits was hard, so she boarded the plane with her heart full of positivity, glowing with good intentions. She buzzed with anticipation of a new, fun adventure, one where somehow she escaped the problems that seemed to be piling higher and higher.

She checked her watch. Twenty-eight hours since the plane took off, and she was still stuck in limbo. She'd been running on adrenaline since the ferry brought her to this tiny rock in the middle of the sea, and fatigue hung on her like a heavy velvet cloak.

What was it Louise always said? Stress is toxic.

Things might not be going her way, but she was here, in a new country, on a new adventure. Everything was new and different. She owed it to herself to enjoy the experience. She swallowed a mouthful of the warm resinous wine, and, despite herself, felt her body relax. The sunshine warmed her skin, and the little iron table and chairs on the pavement outside the cafe looked like they could have come straight from a picture postcard. There weren't many people present—it was too late for lunch and too early for dinner. And all the shops had closed for the day. They seemed to close early on the island, or at least any of the shops she wanted to visit. There was a wide, whitewash-splashed circle on the ground in the corner of the square. She'd noticed a similar ring painted near the port. Curious.

She checked her phone. Still no signal.

The waiter smiled on his way back inside after delivering an amber drink to the neighboring table.

"Excuse me." She batted her eyelashes and smiled as sweetly as she could manage. "Can I hook into the wifi?"

He raised his eyebrows.

"I want to hook...."

"You want to hook up?" A beautiful Greek girl pushed past the waiter to face Ella square-on. She planted her hands on her hips and glared with a look of contempt. "You wish to hook up with Michalis? You're on the island for less than a day and already you're propositioning young men. God, you Americans...." She puffed out a frustrated breath. "He's working. Can you even see that he's working? And you're way too old for him. He could be your son."

There was no fight left in Ella, but she jutted out her chin anyway. No one got to talk to her like this. On this day or any other. "Wifi," she said slowly and deliberately. "I'm trying to download my email, not proposition anyone."

"Oh." The girl had the grace to at least look a little embarrassed. "The internet."

Ella waved her phone. "Yes. The internet. My phone has no signal, and I'm trying to get in contact with someone. My daughter."

The waiter shook his head. "I'm sorry, no internet. Maybe tomorrow."

"Tomorrow?" Ella grimaced. She sank her head into her hands and pushed back her hair. She looked over at the neighboring table. "Can you fetch me a brandy?"

"Okay, I should apologize." The girl pulled out a chair and sat down. "I'm Elena." She cast a glance at the waiter. "Can you bring an orange juice, Michalis?"

He nodded and walked back inside.

"You've had a bad day." It wasn't a question. It was a statement. Ella must look as terrible as she felt. "I was rude, forgive me. What can I do to help you?"

Elena seemed genuine, and life was too short to hold a grudge. Besides, the waiter was hot, and she was only defending her territory. It was sort of flattering, in a weird way, to think that she might have considered Ella as competition.

Where to start? "Have you ever made a split-second decision and regretted it?" It wasn't her first time doing so. Older didn't necessarily mean wiser. While Elena considered the question, Ella continued before she could respond. "My daughter is here for the summer. I decided to surprise her, but she doesn't know I'm coming, and right now, I can't make contact with her."

Not for the first time, the folly of waiting until she arrived in Greece before contacting Amber was hammered home. She couldn't get a signal, so had decided to send an email, but that proved challenging, too. She eyed a pigeon pecking around the base of a nearby table and idly wondered whether sending messages by carrier pigeon had ever been a thing on this island, or did they resort to smoke signals?

Maybe this whole trip was a bad idea.

"I have no service." She held up her phone and rechecked it.

"You need to go to the white circle."

Puzzling over the words didn't help.

"The white circle." Elena pointed across the square to the circle painted on the cobblestones. A woman walking nearby and simultaneously holding up her phone, searching for a signal, moved into the ring. She stopped and pressed the phone to her ear.

"The circles show where the signal is strong. The council repaints them in the summer for the tourists." Elena rubbed the back of her neck. "Where is your daughter staying?"

Ella shrugged. "I don't know."

"But she's working on the island?"

Ella nodded. "On the excavation with her boyfriend. I decided to surprise her, but I can't make contact."

Their drinks arrived, and Elena toasted Ella before downing the glass of orange juice in one gulp.

"There's no cell phone signal at the excavation site. All the volunteers are off duty now and will be heading down to town. Why don't you leave a message and wait for her to contact you? Have a meal. Relax." She glanced around, noting Ella's suitcase and raincoat. "Where are you staying?"

Ella forced a tight smile. "That's another problem."

"Go to the circle and try to contact your daughter. I'll watch your things." Elena leaned back on the chair, stretched out her legs, and crossed them at the ankle.

In the circle, her phone had two bars reception. If Ella took a couple of steps left, she lost them. A couple of steps to the right made them disappear, too. Magic.

A determined-looking twenty-something male strode in her direction, phone gripped in his hand. He edged into the circle standing so close their forearms brushed. He grinned, shrugged his shoulders, jammed the phone to his ear, and spoke in rapid Greek.

Ella held her ground. She typed a quick text: 'Call me when you get this' and sent it.

She was just about to step out of the circle when "Pocket Full of Sunshine" blared from her phone.

"Sorry." She squeezed into the circle again, back to back with the local Adonis. "Amber?"

"Hi, Mom. What's up?"

Excitement sparked through Ella's veins. Amber would be so surprised she was here on the island! In mere minutes they could be together, catching up. And she'd meet Liam—

"Mom? Are you there?"

"Amber, honey. I'm sorry. Yes. Where are you?"

Silence for a moment. Then, "Uh, in my apartment. Why?"

"Not on Kosmima?" She felt faint. She tilted her head back then realized it was brushing against the Adonis's back, so she snapped her head back to level and leaned away. "I thought you traveled to the island on Thursday."

"Oh, we've delayed it for a few days. Flights were cheaper if we waited, so we're heading out the day after tomorrow, and we're taking the opportunity to see some of Greece before we arrive on the island. We're visiting Athens and traveling to another Greek island Liam wants to share with me. We'll be there in about twelve days. Wait, I'll check." A pause then, "Fourth of July. We'll be arriving on Independence Day."

"Ah."

"Is everything okay with you, Mom? I know you're disappointed that I haven't come home, and you may be stressed that I'm going out into the world—traveling to Greece—but Liam will be with me, and I'll be careful of pickpockets and all that stuff."

"Uh-huh." To tell her, or not to tell her? There didn't seem to be any point in revealing that Ella was on the island, especially now. "Well, I just called to see how you were getting on in Greece, honey. Everything is fine with me."

The atmosphere in the circle was getting heated. Her cell-phone circle buddy must be talking to a lover, he was making sounds that really shouldn't be heard outside of the bedroom, and she felt his body heat through the inches that separated their backs.

Ella tugged at the neckline of her tee-shirt. "Okay, I'll let you go and call you again in a few days." She stepped out of the circle and out of coverage.

Elena was still at the table when Ella returned. She lifted her glass. "So, you talked to her! She is meeting you here, yes?"

"No." Ella waved at Michalis, lifted her empty glass, and pointed at it, mouthing, *bring me another*. "No. No. No." Shoot. She'd told Louise she'd be gone for a couple of weeks, but she definitely needed longer. She'd anticipated a couple of weeks to get Liam's father onside and to talk Ella out of getting married and back to college. Now, she'd be on the island for at least three weeks.

There could be worse things than having to spend extra time on a gorgeous Greek island, but right now, the logistics of getting settled were overwhelming.

"I need to find somewhere to stay. I'm going to be here longer than I thought. Probably three weeks or so. Any ideas?" Ella's drink arrived, and she swallowed a mouthful, feeling the burn all the way down.

"Well, there's Twin Pines. That's the only hotel on the island. Some volunteers stay there, the ones who have enough money to book a room instead of staying in the tents." Her nose wrinkled. "I wouldn't stay in one of those tents the students use for anything. It's either too hot, too many insects, or blowing away in a storm. I'd pay the money for a hotel room, and I'm not the only one. You will be lucky if you find a vacant room for three weeks in the hotel."

"What about a B & B?"

Elena looked confused. "Is that a type of drink?"

"I mean, somewhere where they rent out a room. Someone's house. And maybe provide breakfast."

"Ah, bed and breakfast. I understand." Elena smiled. "It's not a problem. Something will work out. The best thing is to go down to Twin Pines and ask Kitten if she has a room available. I'll take you."

# Chapter Six

They chatted on the way. Elena explained how the island didn't have many of the facilities of the larger islands and had much less tourist trade. As such, there weren't many rooms to rent.

"Kosmima is quiet. There are a few places to go to at night, but we don't have nightclubs. And the young like to have places to drink, to talk, to dance, all night." She raised an eyebrow. "A lot of times, bad stuff comes along with that. We don't want that on Kosmima. We don't have enough police to keep the peace."

The sun's heat warmed Ella's shoulders. The streets through the town were rough and cobbled, and many were unsuitable for cars. There were some cars on Kosmima, and it was possible to rent motorbikes and scooters, but for the most part, people walked.

"It must be a strain on the island's resources when the students come for the dig."

"Yes." Elena smiled. "The population almost doubles in the summertime. We have to bring in extra food and supplies from the bigger islands, but the ferry runs twice every day, so that is easy enough. We all work hard when the students arrive. The money they spend while here is a great boost to the economy. It's worth it."

"So during the rest of the year—"

"It's quiet. Deathly quiet. We're a small island without the resources to bring jobs or opportunities. When our young people finish school, they have no option but to leave to go to college or to find work. Some of them come back. But most don't." Her face was somber; her expression serious. "I have two brothers in Athens. They come home for holidays, but living here?" She shrugged. "I can't see them ever returning to the island to live again. There's no work for them here. No way for them to make money."

"Do your parents live here?"

Elena nodded. "There's only my father. My mother died a few years ago." She acknowledged Ella's muttered condolences. "His family have lived on the island for generations. He's a fisherman, just like his father and grandfather before him. The island is in his blood. He'll never leave."

She waved a hand at a large, whitewashed building with a wooden sign hanging outside. *Twin Pines* was painted in flowery black script on a pale pink background. Window boxes filled with masses of bright red and purple flowers decorated each window, and the turquoise blue front door was open to the street.

"Twin Pines. Kitten will help you find somewhere." With a smile and a wave, Elena continued on the road, greeting locals by name and rushing to help someone who must be one of her friends, struggling to carry a baby and a bag of groceries.

Ella couldn't believe she was so ill-informed about Kosmima. She'd done basic research: How to get here. What currency they used. Whether or not she would need a phrasebook. And then she had booked a flight and abandoned home.

She'd been so caught up in the idea of meeting up with

Amber, Liam, and his father she hadn't even been concerned about a hotel room. She'd imagined if there was nothing close to the dig, she could find one further afield, hire a car, and commute. But on this island, the concept of the daily commute was an alien one. And for the first time, the reality of her situation seeped in. Her options were limited if she couldn't find a bed at Twin Pines. So limited, she didn't even know where to begin.

She dragged her suitcase through the open door. It twisted on the step, and one of the wheels fell off.

"Shit!" Ella bent down, picked it up, and shoved it in her handbag. Then, struggling, she maneuvered the suitcase to the reception desk.

"Good afternoon." The receptionist's smile was warm and welcoming. "Welcome to Twin Pines. Are you checking in?"

"Well, here's the thing. I don't have a reservation." Maybe, despite everything Elena insinuated, she didn't need a reservation. Perhaps there had been a last-minute cancellation, and—

The smile slid off the receptionist's face. "Oh, I'm so sorry, we don't have any rooms available. We're fully booked at the moment."

Ella breathed in deep. Forced her smile not to waver. "Elena from the café told me that would probably be the case. She walked me down here and suggested that I talk to Kitten Gataki, and that maybe she would have some suggestions as to where I might find some lodging. I really need some help here."

The receptionist waved to a sofa to the left of the reception area. "Okay, take a seat. I'll get Kitten for you." She hurried into a room behind the reception desk, which probably was a back office.

Ella dragged her suitcase—really, why was her suitcase so frigging heavy? What did she need all this crap for?—to the sofa and sank onto it. What sort of name was Kitten anyway?

It sounded like the name of a cute twenty-something rather than a businesswoman.

"Hi. I'm Kitten." The hotel owner glided to the sofa and sat. Kitten Gataki was small and curvy, with chestnut hair piled on top of her head in an intricate topknot. Large gold hoops hung from her lobes, and she accessorized her plain navy silk shirt with a turquoise choker which matched her pinky ring. Her perfectly manicured long fingernails were painted shell pink. She had the tiniest black beauty mark just above her top lip, so well positioned Ella half wondered if it was painted on. "I hear you need some help finding somewhere to stay." Her smile was so open and welcoming, Ella almost wept with relief.

"Ella Blackstone. And yes, I'm hoping you can save me, Kitten. You're my only hope!" She grinned, but there was no indication that Kitten picked up on her cheesy Princess Leia reference, so she fidgeted, twisting her hands together then sitting on them.

"As you know, we have no rooms available at the moment. How long are you planning to stay on the island?"

"Probably about three weeks." She wanted to launch into a wordy explanation about why she was here, how she'd planned to meet up with Amber and the others, and put her case against her daughter's wedding plans. But explaining it to someone else—even the thought of explaining it to someone else—revealed the gaps in her argument. There were gaping holes in her plan. First, she hadn't even known her daughter wasn't on the island. Second, Amber and Liam must have had their own struggles to get accommodation; it was hardly reasonable to expect to piggyback on their arrangements. And third, once they realized she was anti, rather than pro, the wedding, they probably wouldn't want to have much to do with her anyway.

"Three weeks." Kitten rubbed her chin. "We will have a

room available at the end of next week, but that still gives you two weeks to find accommodation for. A woman rents out a couple of rooms in her house, but they are taken up with students. We have an archaeological dig here every year—"

"I know."

Kitten raised an eyebrow at Ella's harsh tone.

"My daughter is on the dig. She hasn't arrived on Kosmima yet." She forced a tight smile. "It's a long story."

"I have one more possible solution." Kitten observed her keenly. "How do you feel about cats?"

* * *

Ella didn't lie. But she didn't exactly tell the truth either. Which is why she ended up half an hour later sitting in a bedroom with the insistent mewing of a troupe of felines on the other side of the door.

Kitten had explained that the only room she knew that was available was that attached to the Kosmima cat hotel.

"It's a rescue center. The cats are all healthy and half-feral, but they need food and somewhere to stay in bad weather. A team of volunteers look after their needs and fulfill a rota for feeding and cleaning litter boxes and that sort of thing. The apartment is available temporarily for those who stay, in exchange for two hours work a day."

Ella jumped at the opportunity. She'd never found an animal she didn't like. And the fact she was not precisely allergic but definitely sensitive to cat dander had been an unfortunate downside, but not enough to cause her to abandon the solution to her problems.

So now, in the bedroom of the two-room apartment segregated from the rest of the cat hotel, she threw open the glass doors and stepped out onto the narrow iron balcony facing the slopes of the Kosmima hills.

She pressed a wet cloth against her stinging eyes and sneezed a couple of times. It was early evening, but there was no sign of anyone outside. When she questioned Kitten about restaurants where she might be able to get some dinner, Kitten told her they wouldn't open until nine or ten and suggested she stock up on food in the store on the way.

She'd bought basic supplies: wine, water, cheese, bread, olives, and coffee, but the effort of having to prepare anything was too much.

The urgent need to find shelter had kept adrenalin pumping through her veins all day, but now, with the issue resolved, jet lag took over. She'd never felt so exhausted. Too exhausted to even eat.

Ella turned her back on the view. Then she freed the gauzy curtains from their tiebacks, so they swung closed over the open door to the balcony. Then she stumbled to the large iron bed, slipped off her sandals, and collapsed on top of the colorful patchwork quilt.

* * *

It was dark when Ella woke. Impossible to make out anything in the velvet blackness of the room, and for a long moment, she lay disorientated, unsure where she was, what time of day it could be.

Kosmima.

She sat up in bed. Patted down her pockets and the bed but couldn't locate her phone. She recalled a vague memory of a table beside the bed with a light and continued her patting to the mattress's edge. After a gap, her questing fingers located a hard wooden surface and then a lamp. She flicked it on, releasing the breath she hadn't even been aware of holding.

The sound of music flowed in through the open window.

Ella walked to the billowing curtain and stepped out onto

the balcony to hear it better. It was familiar—something she hadn't heard for years and years. Not since she was a student. Her mouth curved into a smile. Something about the music recalled fun nights. Dancing.

What was that tune?

"Livin' la Vida Loca."

Ella gasped.

A male voice sang her the answer. But not just any male voice—a voice she knew. She gripped the iron balcony rail, barely registering that it was cold beneath her fingers now the heat of the sun was gone. It couldn't be. Her ears strained to hear the voice again over the burble of voices wafting up from the taverna next door. The chorus swelled, and now everyone seemed to be singing along. The sound of that original voice, the karaoke singer wielding the microphone, was drowned out by the crowd.

Ella stepped back into the room. She closed the door and let the curtain fall back in place. Then she shoved her feet into her sandals, grabbed her keys, and dashed outside.

The street was pretty deserted, but people spilled out of the open door of the taverna. She stepped inside, weaving back and forth through the bodies filling the space. There were small round tables in the middle of the room with people sitting at them.

Around the periphery people stood holding drinks, and at one end of the room was a long bar, with every bar stool occupied. There was barely enough room to move, but everyone in the room seemed to be having a good time. The atmosphere was electric.

At the far end of the room was a karaoke set-up, and the mysterious musician was still Ricky Martining his way through "Livin' la Vida Loca".

The room, the people in it, all peripheral details, faded into a blur as Ella's focus lasered on the singer. It was him.

There was no grey in the familiar mop of curly hair she'd tugged with her fingers, but the rest of him had changed. Had aged, but not in a bad way. At nineteen, he'd been tall and thin. His shoulders had filled out over the past twenty years, and his body added some weight. Back then, he'd been a beautiful boy. Now he was all man.

He rotated his hips. Grinned—the dimples were still there—and the crowd laughed and clapped.

Aidan Dempsey. A man she deliberately stopped thinking about twenty years ago when she got on that plane and flew out of Ireland. The man who never crossed her mind, unless she had drunk too much and allowed herself to wallow in what could have been, what might have been, had things been different.

He finished the song with a flourish. Bowed to a table at the front left, and the table's occupants raised their glasses to him as he bounded off the stage back to them. His friends.

Kitten Gataki sat with a gorgeous man-mountain playing close attention to her and another woman, who smiled up at Aidan as though he was a visiting film star.

He reached for a pint of beer on the table. Picked it up. His gaze scanned the room. Then he looked straight at Ella.

She hadn't recognized him straight away. And she'd been looking for him because she heard his voice. She'd changed enough in twenty years to be pretty sure he wouldn't know her at a glance, but he didn't look away.

The smile fell from his face. He just stood there, staring.

His female companion said something. He didn't respond. She followed his gaze to where Ella stood transfixed, and a frown marred her features. She spoke again. He still didn't look away. Instead, he frowned and mouthed *Trouble*?

Her heart pounded. There was a roomful of people between them, but her focus was entirely on Aidan. The distance of space and time contracted until it was just as it had been the last time she saw him. When they looked at each other and the entire world faded and blurred, as if there was no one in the room but the two of them.

The urge was strong to run away. Instead, she raised a hand and wiggled her fingers.

* * *

It was as though Aidan were having an out-of-body experience. As though he'd traveled through a time tunnel, or spun into a time vortex. Singing Ricky Martin had been such a blast from the past; maybe this time, he'd actually lost his mind for real.

"Aidan." Kitten tugged his sleeve, diverting his attention from the apparition across the room.

He glanced over. Glanced back to see if the ghost from his past was still there.

"Aidan," Kitten hissed. She signaled with her eyes to the woman at his side. The woman he was supposed to be on a first date with. He didn't know Sophia well, but there was no mistaking the pissed-off look in her eyes.

"I'm sorry. It's someone I knew a long time ago...."

Kitten looked at him as though he was crazy, and Nick shook his head with his mouth twisted in a grimace. A look he knew well. The 'oh-fuck-stop-now' look.

Aidan looked back. A flood of panic overtook him when he couldn't see the woman, then subsided as he saw her striding to the bar. The way she walked—who knew the way she moved would be so familiar after this many years?

"I'm sorry, but I have to go and speak to someone." He leaned down, gripped Sophia's upper arms, and kissed her on both cheeks. "I knew her years ago. I have to find out why... how she's here." He fixed his gaze on Nick. "Get the girls another drink; I'll be back as soon as I can."

"You don't want to bring her over?" Nick looked desperate.

Aidan shook his head slowly. "Sorry, man."

"Go." Sophia pouted. "It's fine." It didn't sound fine.

"The American?" Kitten was looking at the bar. At Trouble.

"You know her?"

"She arrived on the island today. She didn't say she was looking for you—she was looking for a room."

"Okay." He could stand around here pumping Kitten for information, or he could get across the room to her before she disappeared. Shit, Nick would give him hell in the morning, but there was nothing he could do about that. He grabbed his jacket from the back of the chair and walked away from the table.

She stood with her back to the bar.

She was holding a glass of red wine.

The echoes of the girl she'd been were evident in her face today, an older face, but one no less lovely than it had been. The ghost of his past—the one that got away—gazed at him with wide, cornflower blue eyes. Her full mouth curved into a welcoming smile. Her honey-blonde hair was shorter, shoulder-length now, rather than halfway down her back as it had been back in Dublin.

He stopped in front of her. Let his gaze wander from her head to toe. Dark denim jeans clung to her curves like a second skin, and a cherry-red shirt showed a glimpse of cleavage.

"There's only one man in the world who sings 'Livin' la Vida Loca' like that. And it's not Ricky." The smile started small, just a twitch at the corners of her lips, then widened to a full-on grin. Then she was laughing, and he was, too. Both of them caught up in the moment. The incredible, bizarre coincidence that they should meet now on this desolate rock in the middle of the ocean.

"Ella." He hadn't felt his mouth shape her name for decades. "Fuckin' hell, Ella, what are you doing here?"

Music built—a touch of Queen, by the sound of it—and a drunken couple of men stepped onto the stage and took the mics hostage.

"Let's talk outside."

She brushed against him on the way out of the door. A faint scent of her perfume floated in the night breeze as she passed, jolting him back twenty years. There were tables set up —one of them empty—but he didn't want to sit at a table with her while Nick, Sophia, and Kitten were inside. It was bad enough that he'd dumped his date for another woman. He didn't need to rub her nose in it.

"I'm sorry—I didn't mean to intrude on your evening. I should meet your partner. Explain how we know each other."

"She's not my partner. I was on a first date."

She winced. Aidan knew just how she felt. He looked left and right, considering where they could go.

"Come on." She glanced back over her shoulder to make sure he was following, then walked to a dark-blue front door he'd never really noticed before, and opened it with a key she took from her pocket.

"I'm staying here." She grabbed his arm and pulled him quickly inside. "Close the door quick. I can't let the cats out."

"Cats?"

Ella flicked on the light.

Aidan glanced around. Thirty or so pairs of eyes gazed back. Cats everywhere. On the floor, on the chairs, every available surface seemed to be decorated with a living, furry being. They stared at him as though they could tell he was a 'dog man.'

"This is weird." This day was getting stranger and stranger by the minute.

"It is. Immensely weird. Come on." She took his hand and

led him through the house, explaining as they went that she had no alternative but to stay in the cat sanctuary because there were no rooms available anywhere else. He barely followed the gist of her story. There were too many felines to avoid tripping over. "They're not allowed in here." She stood outside a door. "Open, then dash. Right?"

"Got it."

"I'll go first, then you. Be quick."

He glanced around. Three cats nearby. They didn't look interested in storming the door, but cats were unpredictable, prone to darting, so he dashed through after Ella and shoved the door closed before they could try anything.

Their bodies collided in the darkness.

"Don't move. I'll get the light."

A minute later, a bedside lamp spilled a pool of golden light into the room.

The strains of "Bohemian Rapsody" drifted in from the open door from the balcony. She lowered herself onto the bed, and he found the only chair in the room and sat, too.

"That's how you heard me."

"Yes."

"But how? I don't understand. How can you possibly be here?"

"You're a professor now? Professor Dempsey?"

"Yes," he snapped back, impatient. His title meant nothing, had nothing to do with this situation, and he had no interest in wasting time on pleasantries.

"I'm here for you." She scrunched up her eyes and pulled a face. "Argh. I mean, I'm here to meet with you, although I never in my wildest dreams thought you and Professor Dempsey were the same person. Would you like some wine?"

"Sure."

"I'll be back in a minute." She dashed out of the door, then reappeared a few moments later clutching two glasses and a bottle of red. “I thought the cats would settle down at night, but they were all lurking there ready to party.”

She poured them both a glass and placed the bottle on the table.

One of the cats yowled outside the door.

“You have a child.” It sounded like a statement rather than a question.

“I married straight out of college. We had a son.”

“I have a daughter. She’s in Trinity.”

“You live...where?”

“Monterey. Do you remember my grandfather’s educational fund paid for me to go to Trinity? Well, it’s doing the same for Amber.”

“Amber.” Gears clicked in his head. An American girl called Amber. Oh no, she couldn’t possibly mean...

She nodded.

“Liam’s girlfriend.”

His ex’s daughter was his son’s girlfriend. There sounded something horribly wrong about that. And what were the odds? His mind churned over everything Liam had said about Amber. Why hadn’t he paid more attention? Did they know? It hardly seemed possible that either of their children knew about their past.

Ella walked over and filled up both of their glasses. “That’s only the half of it.”

“They’re coming out to stay at the beginning of July—but I guess you know that. Liam didn’t say anything about you joining them, though.” He eyed her carefully, taking in the play of different emotions across her face. “What the hell’s going on, Trouble?”

“I haven’t been Trouble for twenty years.”

Aidan felt one of his eyebrows rise as he eyed her. “I doubt that.” He grinned.

“It’s a long story.” She bit the corner of her lip. Frowned.

For once in her life, it appeared that the woman he'd christened Trouble was speechless.

"I had no idea Amber was in a relationship with your son. No clue. I came to talk to Liam's father, but I had no idea Professor Dempsey and you were the same person. There are thousands of Dempseys in Ireland. Hundreds of thousands." She swallowed another mouthful of wine. She looked at him, really looked. "I can't believe it's you."

Aiden tumbled backward through time to the last moment he'd seen her. His day's lectures over, he'd spotted her waving at him from across the quad as he dashed for the front gate.

He'd been running for a bus—going home for the weekend. He'd told his parents about her that weekend and had promised to bring the American he was dating with him to meet them soon.

What an idiot he'd been.

Aidan swallowed the last of his wine. Glanced at his watch. "I have to get back to my date. But you and I need to talk. I'll be here tomorrow morning. Early. You can tell me this long story then."

# Chapter Seven

It felt like an alternate universe. One in which the years she'd spent living with Jason, running *Precious Things*, and being a mother, wife, and businesswoman faded to grey.

She'd been carefree a long time ago. So long ago, she'd almost forgotten. It was logical to expect that Aidan might not have even recognized her when he saw her across the room in the taverna. She might not even have recognized him if she hadn't heard him singing.

She would have noticed him, that was for sure. He was a good-looking man. Different to how he'd been in his late teens; his body was more filled out, his lean build solidified into muscle no doubt earned from carting away loads of soil and rock while excavating. And he had lines at the corners of his eyes. As she did.

The yowling of the cats woke her just after dawn. She fed them, cleaned any litter boxes that needed cleaning, and replenished their food and water bowls. Aidan had said he'd call for her early; she wanted to be ready.

He rapped on the door at eight, took one look at her, and frowned. "Have you been crying?"

Ella's eyes felt red and irritated. A reminder she should find a chemist and pick up some antihistamines.

She shook her head. "Cats. I'm sensitive to cat hair. I'll be fine. Some coffee?" She stood back to allow him entry, but he declined.

"I brought breakfast. Let's sit outside."

She grabbed her bag and pulled the door shut behind her.

Next door, tables were set up outside the closed taverna, so they sat. Aidan emptied the contents of his daypack onto the table. A paper bag with pastries. A thermos flask and two plastic travel cups. He poured a cup of steaming coffee from the flask and helped himself to a pastry dusted with flaked almonds.

"White, no sugar okay?" He glanced over, eyebrow raised.

"Just the way I like it."

He poured the second cup.

"I'm impressed." She scratched at an irritated, red patch of skin under her ear, then she sipped the coffee and bit into a pastry.

"Don't be. I pick breakfast up from the café. Elena just doubled my order this morning." He eyed her carefully. Everything about him was different today. Last night, he'd been unguarded, surprised to see her. He'd obviously been thinking about things, considering just why she was here.

Ella chewed. She tried not to be intimidated by his close regard. She hadn't done anything wrong—she was only doing what any concerned mother would do.

"They don't know you're here, do they?"

"Uh..."

"Your daughter and my son don't know you are here, do they?"

Had his eyes always been that blue? Aidan's mouth was set

in a straight line, and there was a crease between his eyebrows. He'd make a good interrogator. The urge to either confess or run away was overwhelming.

"No, they don't."

His frown deepened. "So you're one of those helicopter mothers. One who is unhappy about her daughter dating an unsuitable boy." His mouth flattened. A muscle flexed in the corner of his jaw. "She's in university, Ella. She's allowed to fall in love."

"You think I don't know that?" How could he, of all people, lecture her about falling in love? She'd been three-quarters of the way to falling in love with him when her mother and father dragged her out of Trinity and shoved her on the plane back to the States.

He shrugged. "I'm just working on the evidence of my own eyes. You've never even met Liam. And you didn't know he was my son?" He leaned forward. "Is that true? Did you really not know?"

"I was just as clueless as you that our children were dating."

He ran his hand through his hair in a gesture that was instantly familiar, even though she hadn't seen him do it for years.

"I don't have anything against Liam. I'm sure he's a great guy. And I have no problem with Amber falling in love and having boyfriends, even living with them if she wants to. This is the twenty-first century. I'm not a prude. I'm a realist."

"So why the hell have you decided to fly across the world to crash their summer? This isn't a fun holiday, you know. When they arrive, I expect them to work. We start early every morning—" He checked his watch and crumpled the empty paper bag that had contained the pastries— "which reminds me, I'll have to go in a couple of minutes."

"I know that. I applied to volunteer, but there were no places available." He drained his coffee. She needed to keep this conversation going; he couldn't walk away without understanding what was at stake. But at the same time, she couldn't just come right out and tell him their kids were planning to get married either. Amber had said they were coming here expressly to break the news. If she pre-empted that, her daughter would be so angry there would be no chance of talking her around.

"Can I come with you? To the dig?"

His eyebrows rose. Then his blue eyes scanned Ella's body. Head to toe. "You're not exactly dressed for it."

She'd thrown on a printed cotton wrap dress that floated to mid-calf and a pair of cherry-red kitten heels.

"It'll take me five minutes to change. Come on, Aidan. Give me a break. You don't know everything. We need to talk through this."

"I have a team of volunteers to supervise. Work to do."

She showed him her palms. "I can work. I need to come with you." She crossed her arms.

His expression softened. It started with a look in his eyes, then the corner of his mouth twitched, and in a split second, he was smiling.

"I'd forgotten how stubborn you could be."

She grinned back. "I was Trouble, remember?"

"Okay, you can come. But you'll have to work for the entire day. I don't have time to walk you back down the hill after an hour or so. And we'll have to fit in time to talk when it's convenient." He stowed the flask and coffee cups into the day pack. "Which won't be until later. Nick and I have a lot of work to do today. We have politicians visiting the site tomorrow."

"Nick. Was he the guy you were with last night?"

He nodded.

Kitten's date. The guy who had looked between her and Aidan with open curiosity in his gaze.

"Run up and get changed, then we'll go." Aidan slung the bag over his shoulder. "Wear sneakers."

* * *

Being with her, here and now, felt surreal. The trek up the hill to the encampment was rocky but not steep. Aidan had walked it so often he paid little attention to the sights on the way. But Ella seemed captivated. She stopped to examine plants that grew wild on the verges. She picked sprigs of dark purple flowered rosemary and crushed other herbs between her fingers, breathing in their scent as she moved. She examined each tree and questioned him if she couldn't identify the species.

The years had been good to her. She looked different, but not in a bad way. He'd been drawn to her the moment he first met her in the college bar, and now, decades later, that old familiar attraction zinged in the air between them.

"Amber told me you're a widower. I'm sorry."

He never knew what the correct answer to that should be. *It's fine*, wasn't true, and *thank you* sounded insincere and empty. So Aidan responded as he usually did, with a curt nod and a rapid subject change.

"And you're divorced?"

"Divorced for six months, yes." She kicked a stone and shoved her hands deep into the front pockets of her jeans. "I think my ex-husband Jason is planning on marrying the woman he left me for." She frowned. "She's ten years younger and ten pounds lighter."

"And probably ten times less interesting."

Her mouth curved in a Mona Lisa smile. "You always were able to make me feel better."

"It was a long time ago. We were different people."

"I don't feel different." She pushed her sunglasses up onto the top of her head; fixed him with a defiant stare. "I guess if anything, I feel muted, compared to the intensity of my emotions when I was younger, but I still feel the same, inside. Don't you?"

Aidan stopped. He turned to face her. Her eyes. Her mouth. The tiny mole on her left cheek, below the outer corner of her eye. Once upon a time, his mouth had pressed over that little mark. She would laugh, and he would kiss her again. She'd always laughed. Would she now?

The desire to find out was overwhelming.

"Ella." He stepped close and rubbed the pad of his thumb over the curve of her jawline. Her chest rose with a quick intake of breath. Her pupils expand in a telling response to his touch. The attraction between them was still there—as electric as ever.

Somehow, after an entire lifetime lived apart, it still survived.

"You might feel the same as you were then. But you're not. And neither am I." He looked deliberately at her mouth—let his gaze linger. "We didn't work then; we wouldn't work now."

She sucked in a startled breath. Then took a hurried step back, almost tripping on the rough scree. "I wasn't trying to—
"

"Good." He glanced up the hill, then back. "We better pick up the pace. The volunteers will be at the campsite already."

She muttered as she followed, but he tuned her out. Ella had been able to manipulate him as easily as breathing. He hadn't known that was what she was doing back then. He'd thought she felt the same as he did, that she was as helplessly enmeshed in their teen love as he was. But she wasn't. Because if she were, she never would have tossed the grenade into their relationship, ensuring its total and utter destruction.

Hopefully, her daughter wouldn't do the same to his son.

Liam was like his mother, a total romantic. He believed in happy ever after and fell in love so quickly he'd met 'the love of his life' approximately every six months since he was sixteen. Helping out at the dig two years ago as a schoolboy, before he'd even got into college, he'd started a great romance with the daughter of Betty Milthrop, one of Aidan's colleagues.

Betty was back this year. He'd forgotten to check if her daughter Janice was attending this year, too. She'd gone to university in Scotland, hadn't she?

"Do you think you could slow down?" A call from behind him.

He stopped.

Ella ran the last few steps to catch up. He started walking again, slower this time.

"I'm here for my daughter. I didn't even know you were here."

"I know." He'd given her hell because he wasn't ready, wasn't expecting the attraction that burst into life so suddenly. He wasn't a teenager any longer, wasn't someone who ever had thoughts of hot, sweaty sex force their way into his mind and take over. He was a grown-up. Spending time with a woman was something to be considered, evaluated, and savored. Something planned and enjoyed by both parties. The women he slept with knew the score. They knew he wasn't interested in anything serious. Or a long-term relationship.

But that moment. Today. With the feel of Ella's skin under his fingertips, he'd been almost seduced by an impulse. There had been signs of awareness shifting into arousal on her face and in her body, and he hadn't been immune. He'd wanted to kiss her, so he shut down desire before he could do anything stupid. That wasn't his fault, but it wasn't her fault either.

The faint sound of voices and laughter carried in the wind.

An encampment of small white tents set into the foothills of the hillside came into view. A thin stream of smoke curled into the air.

"We're here."

* * *

The dig was fun. Everyone had a mission, and the enthusiasm of the young volunteers was infectious. As warned, Aidan was busy, so Ella wandered around, checking out the various excavation sites and watching what everyone was doing.

She'd spent time on a dig after college, so the procedures were familiar. And the prospect of finding something, uncovering a fragment of pottery, or perhaps a flint arrowhead, made her wish she'd been able to sign in as a volunteer.

"Are you just a tourist, or are you here to work?" A woman on her knees in a trench addressed Ella.

"I'd like to work, but I wasn't able to sign on as a volunteer. All the places were taken."

The woman got to her feet and brushed red earth from the knees of her chinos. "Today could be your lucky day." She climbed out of the trench. Extended a hand. "Betty Milthrop."

Ella introduced herself.

"You came up with Aidan."

"Yes, we're...um...."

One of Betty's eyebrows rose. "It's none of my business."

"You've got the wrong—"

"Like I said, none of my business. If you're just waiting around, that's fine, but if you were serious about wanting to work, I could do with the help. I was supposed to have four volunteers helping me in this trench, but only two turned up today. The others could be sick, hungover...or worse, disenchanted. Unfortunately, about thirty-percent drop out shortly after getting here and decide to holiday on the island instead."

"I haven't done this for a long time—"

"Follow me." Betty waved in the direction of a large plastic container underneath a trestle table a few feet away. She gave Ella a selection of tools: a large trowel, with the tip flattened to a point, a wooden skewer, a dustpan, a medium-sized paint-brush, and a bottle of water. "These will be a good start."

Betty was an excellent teacher. She introduced Ella to her two attending students, Sharon and Paolo, and then focused all her attention on bringing Ella up to speed. She clearly and carefully explained how to proceed in excavating the site and demonstrated her technique for scraping away at the earth to reveal any artifacts. "All the earth is to be placed into the zambeli." She touched a large rubber bucket placed close to all the three working areas in the trench. "Once it's half full, one of us will transfer the soil to the wheelbarrow and take it to be screened." She took one look at Ella's face and grinned. "You're concentrating very hard."

"There's a lot to remember; I don't want to do anything wrong."

Betty slapped her on the back. "Don't worry. I'm working right next to you. Start clearing. Let me know if you find anything, and I'll talk you through each next stage. And don't forget to drink your water. It's easy to become dehydrated in this heat."

The four members of Betty's team worked in companionable silence, occasionally stopping to show each other their discoveries and dump the contents of their dustpans into the zambeli. After an hour or two, another student appeared, apologizing profusely, and took up another position in the grid. There was something primal and grounded, working with such close focus to the earth beneath her fingers.

"Can I take Ella off your hands for a while, Betty?" A slice of shade fell over Ella. She looked up to see the outline of Aidan, his features dark in the shadow of the sunlight.

"Sure. But bring her back, please. She's doing good work."

Ella placed her tools down carefully on the ground in a tidy pile and stepped out of the trench.

"I'm sorry it took me so long to come back to you, but it looks as though you've kept yourself busy."

"Yes. I managed to get my hands dirty." She brushed her palms against her jeans. "Some of the volunteers didn't turn up today. Betty's loss was my gain. I was glad to get the chance to do some work."

"She doesn't suffer fools. You must be doing something right. Come on; I'll show you around."

Ella couldn't decide whether his 'you must be doing something right' was sarcastic or not. And didn't care. It was a beautiful day, a magical place, and she'd found a deep and satisfying peace working in nature. She watched volunteers pushing wheelbarrows to the screen station with interest.

Aidan explained how they shoveled soil onto a metal screen suspended above a vat of water, then poured water over the earth, flushing the soil through the screen and leaving small fragments exposed on the screen's surface.

His finger traced through the debris, then he picked up a miniature shard and held it before her. "A fragment of pottery. There was a house here." He looked out across the scrubby brushland. "The view must have been very much the same as it is today."

She held out her hand, and he placed it into her palm. The shard had been buried under the earth for maybe hundreds of years. No one had touched it except her and Aidan since it was dropped and forgotten. She shivered.

"Cold?" He examined her closely.

"Just feeling the brush of history. Ghosts."

Aidan smiled. "Yes, I feel that every day. It's one of the

things I love about this job. Do you remember we used to talk about how everything is interconnected?"

She did. Memories of the nights and days they'd talked about anything and everything flooded into her mind in an inescapable flood.

Ella picked the fragment from her palm and handed it to him. "I guess you better put this with the rest for safekeeping." She brushed her palms down her jeans and avoided his eyes.

"Join me in the tent. We need to talk."

# Chapter Eight

She was messing with his head. Again. Much as Aidan wanted to put aside the feelings that being with Ella brought to the surface, he couldn't. The way she looked at the little piece of pottery, the way she talked about history, had reawakened unwanted memories.

He'd repressed disturbing emotions in the past, but now he didn't have the time or the inclination to sublimate anything. He was still affected by what happened between them twenty years ago. Now that she was on the island, he owed it to himself to deal with the issue while he had the chance.

They walked into the calm sanctuary the tent provided, and he fixed them two cups of black coffee from the thermos flasks set up on a table inside the door.

"Let's talk." He handed a cup over so she could add whatever she wanted to it and then walked to a circle of deckchairs in the rest area. "There are things unsaid between us. About our past. I guess some people would say I should just let it lie, but I've never been one to—"

"Listen to anyone else?" She smiled.

"Run from a difficult situation," he said pointedly, noting that his barb hit its target when she winced.

"We haven't seen each other in over twenty years. I don't see the point in raking up old coals." She sipped coffee. "You made your decision, and I'm fine with it. Really. We both went on to have good lives with other people. We should leave our history in the past."

His decision? He'd made his decision? Aidan couldn't hold back a humorless laugh.

Ella's eyes widened.

"You may be fine with running out on me, vanishing without a trace, but I'm not." He planted his hands on his hips. "It devastated me then, and twenty years later, I'm still annoyed about the way you treated me. So don't go telling me anything was a decision I made. You took away any option I had of making a decision and never looked back."

Okay, that was harsh. More than harsh...brutal. The emotion that welled up from the center of Aidan's being was stronger and more bitter than he imagined it could be after so many years. He had been over her abandonment decades ago, hadn't given her a moment's thought since.

Aidan rubbed the back of his neck and acknowledged the harsh truth. That wasn't exactly true. He'd been melancholy for a few months after she left. Despondent at any mention of her name. His friends had taken to referring to Ella in code as 'the one that got away'.

He hadn't thought he'd ever get over her but, six months later, had started a romance with another Trinity student, Carol. She eventually became his wife. There wasn't any unfinished business between him and Ella. So why did it feel like there was?

"Aidan." Her voice was husky, and a frown creased between her eyebrows.

"It doesn't matter. It was a long time ago. Forget I said

anything." He swallowed a mouthful of coffee and refilled his cup.

She reached out and touched his arm. "No. We have to talk about this." She took in a shaky breath. "I left you a message. My parents took me away and put me straight on a plane back to the States. They didn't even allow me to pack. I was panicking in the accommodation block, and a girl I barely knew told me to write a letter that she would pass on to you. She was in one of the same societies as me, and said she'd seen us together."

There was desperation in her voice, and the expression on her face was earnest and genuine.

"I never got any message."

She pressed a hand to her mouth.

"I called you. Left messages. You never replied to any of them." Revisiting the past opened an ache in his chest. Revived the memory of past hurt, past pain. It was humiliating to remember just how much he'd loved her. Just how special he thought their relationship was. He'd tried to find her address from the college authorities had done everything he could to find her until the cold hard truth sank in. She'd left his life as abruptly as she entered it.

"I..."

It wasn't fair to dump his twenty-year gripes on her.

* * *

The sound of heavy footsteps, then the stiff canvas door of the large tent was pulled back, and Nick walked in.

"We're breaking for lunch." He walked over to the stack of plastic boxes containing plates and picked it up. "You want to help me get ready?" He looked from one to the other with keen interest. What had Aidan told his friend of their past? Had he said anything?

Ella rubbed the back of her neck. Avoided Aidan's eyes. "What can I take?" she asked.

"Silverware." Nick jerked his head in the direction of another large plastic box.

"I'll bring the food." Aidan aimed for the large refrigerator against the far wall.

Ella hefted the box of silverware and headed out into the sunlight.

A couple of volunteers shook the folds from dark blue cotton tablecloths and placed them on the two long tables set up under the olive trees. Ella followed Nick's lead and put the box on the end of the table.

Betty joined them. "Thirty-two." She smiled at Ella's confused expression. "There are thirty-two of us here today. We need to set thirty-two places." She reached into the box for knives and forks and laid them on the left side of the table.

Ella did the same opposite.

"The sun is too high to work now. After lunch, we'll go back to the village for siesta. Some of the volunteers will return for a couple of hours in the late afternoon, but it's not mandatory, so many of them don't make it." She accepted a stack of plates from Nick, shared them with Ella, and put them in place on the table, too.

"I can come back if you like...."

Betty shook her head. "No need, dear. I'll just be logging items and working on paperwork. I'm sure you have more important things to be doing." She glanced across the dusty clearing to where Aidan stood, oblivious. He talked with a group as they set out the food on the adjacent table.

"I will not be doing that." The words escaped before Ella had a chance to self-censor.

Betty burst out laughing.

Embarrassment rose like beer dumped straight into a glass rather than carefully poured down the side. Ella's cheeks were so hot she must be puce. Then she caught Betty's eye, and an answering laugh bubbled up from somewhere.

"It's not as though—" Betty couldn't get the words out.

"It's not as though he's a disaster. Because he's not; he's gorgeous." Ella grinned. "But I've told you once. I won't tell you again. I will not be doing that."

Betty started to laugh again, then shook her head. She rolled her lips in and pressed them hard together. Then, steadied, she took a deep breath and said: "Time's a-wasting. We should eat."

Ella loaded up her plate with a Greek salad of tomatoes, black olives, feta, and a hunk of fresh bread, and took a place at the table. Aidan sat next to her, and Betty dropped in opposite. "Water?"

She nodded, and he poured them both a glass.

"Why are you really here? I'm finding it difficult to believe you're such a helicopter mother you have to hover over your daughter's first relationship with someone you don't know." He popped an olive into his mouth and chewed. "The Trouble I knew would never do that."

Ella frowned. "Amber's just a kid. It's the first time she's been away from home...."

"Just like you when we were together." He looked at her mouth, then back up to her eyes. She'd seen him look at her like that before. Not for a long time, but the response in her body was as heated and fast as though it were yesterday. "You were the same age as she is, and it was the first time either of us had been away from home, too."

She nodded.

"We might have been young, but that didn't make what we felt for each other any less valid. Any less real."

"I know. I just don't want Amber to make a mistake."

His eyebrows rose. "My son is no mistake." His shoulders stiffened. His mouth tightened.

"I didn't mean—I just don't want them going too fast."

"You've talked to her about sex? She knows about birth control?" There was no hint of the warm, flirtatious man she'd been melting in the presence of just seconds ago. "Because beyond that, I don't think you should have an opinion on who your daughter spends her time with. If he or his family were strangers, I could understand you feeling reticent, but you know now. You know he's my son. So you can back off and quit butting in to their relationship."

*Wow*. Ella bit back the words that threatened to escape. The facts that Aidan didn't know, but once he did, would justify her attitude. He didn't know that Amber and Liam planned marriage. She'd promised herself she wouldn't let that information slip. She forked a mouthful of food and looked across the table. Betty's gaze flittered from Ella to Aidan and back again.

Oh great. Their discussion—disagreement—had been noticed.

She was vaguely aware of Aidan focusing his attention on the person to his right. A glance revealed it was Nick.

"Where are you staying?" Betty asked.

"At a cat refuge. And as someone who's not a cat person, all I can say is that it's the very last place I imagined when I booked this trip." She poured a glass of wine for Betty from the bottle in the middle of the table, then topped up her glass.

"I have so many questions." The corners of Betty's mouth curved in a smile. Her gaze flitted to Aidan again.

"It's a long, long story."

"How about coming out to dinner with me tonight? Or maybe you have plans?"

Jet lag was catching up with Ella. "I'm exhausted. I bought some basic supplies, and I'm going to eat in and go to bed early." She forced a tight smile. "Thanks for the offer, though. I'd love to take you up on it some other time."

* * *

"It's difficult to anticipate how many more seasons excavating the site will take." Aidan shuffled the plans on his desk. "It could be as few as two, but if we have a significant find, it could be longer."

Nick stretched his long legs beneath the table. "We have everything ready for the visit tomorrow. I hear the Akrotiri team has a new excavation budget they're dying to spend. I know you're constrained to summer because of your lecturing job, but I plan to take on more projects this year and next."

Aidan spread a map on the desk and pointed. "We have the preliminary plans for these three islands and our standard approach mapped out. We need to survey them in the next few weeks." Aidan closed his laptop. "We've run the numbers and detailed budget fundamentals. There will be more work to do, but first, we need to persuade them that we're the right people to run the excavations."

Nick rolled up the map. "I'm glad the couple from the museum are attending."

After so many years working on Kosmima, Aidan and Nick had built a good reputation, but expert specialists who would vouch for them were always welcome.

Aidan was stowing the documents into his satchel when Nick spoke again. "She's got under your skin, this woman."

He hadn't had a chance to talk to Ella after snapping at her during lunch. She'd left the table while he and Nick were talking. On looking for her, Aidan had discovered she had returned to the village.

"She has that effect, yes."

"Only on you, I think. She seemed to be getting on great with everyone else."

"Our history gets in the way." He'd filled Nick in on all the details while they worked. "And it doesn't help that her daughter is dating Liam."

"I guess Liam thinks he's in love. But that wouldn't be the first time, and it won't be the last either. That boy is a romantic to his core. I don't know where he gets it from." With a wide grin, Nick stowed his laptop in his backpack.

"Me neither."

"How do you feel, seeing her again?" Nick pulled back the canvas doorway and stepped out of the tent.

"I don't know. Nothing much of anything."

It was a lie, and no doubt Nick knew it. Aidan had been unsettled ever since he saw Ella in the taverna. Long-buried feelings: attraction, desire, and anger, had come to the surface again. He was increasingly conflicted by the warring desires of wanting to kiss her and wanting to stay as far away from her as possible.

"You coming for a drink later?"

She lived right next door to the bar. He had been out of line, snapping at her earlier. He should try and smooth things over; he owed that much to Liam. But his shoulders ached, and he yearned for a long, hot shower followed by a quiet meal and a beer. Putting some distance between them would be wise.

"I'll take a rain check."

They picked their way through the stones and straggly shrubland of the hillside on their way back to the village in companionable silence. What was Trouble's daughter like? Was she a firebrand like her mother had been?

Ella must have married Amber's father a year after dropping out of college.

She had married young. Just as Aidan had. Memories flooded back. He and Carol married when they were only a year or so older than Liam was now.

He didn't regret anything about their teenage marriage. Or

about being a father while all his friends were out drinking and chatting up girls every night.

But he and Carol were different. She was pregnant, and they'd made the decision together to get married and make it work. The moment she told him that her period was late, and that she had to take a pregnancy test, and asked him to be there while she waited for the result to show on the stick was the most sobering moment of his life.

Until then, he'd been a teenager in a fun relationship with the second girl he'd ever slept with. College life was great; he'd got himself together after the disaster of the year before when the girl he thought himself in love with disappeared without a trace, and the future stretched out before him like the wide, bright, yellow brick road.

The future was wide open.

The great unknown. Anything was possible. Until it wasn't.

The moment he learned Carol was pregnant, a whole wealth of opportunities vanished. Sure, they were replaced with the chance to devote himself entirely to being a husband and a father. To enjoy closeness and a deep connection with Carol, the only other person who could understand what being a teenage parent was like.

He wouldn't—couldn't—regret anything about his past. It had brought him a deep love for his wife and child. But life had been more challenging once they were parents, and he and Carol often talked about it over the years, and agreed that if she hadn't been pregnant, they would have waited a couple of years before settling down.

The great unsaid between them was that if she'd never become pregnant, maybe both of them might have made different choices.

# Chapter Nine

Ella opened her eyes to warm sunlight streaming through the gauzy lace curtains.

She stepped out of bed and opened the glass door onto the balcony. Vibrant pink bougainvillea snaked up the trellis near her head, and she snapped off a flower and tucked it behind her ear. If she hurried through her cat-related tasks, she could be at the café, making a call from a painted circle before Louise went to bed in the States.

Less than an hour later, at the café, she finished a slice of bread slathered with delicious honey, swallowed a mouthful of coffee, then stepped out into the sunshine with her phone.

Louise answered right away. "Hey, stranger!" There was a buzz of conversation around her. "Hang on. I'm in a bar. I'll just go somewhere quieter." The sound of a door opening and closing, then Louise's familiar voice continued. "So, how's Amber? Did you manage to talk her round yet?"

"Amber and Liam aren't here. They decided to take the scenic route. They're in Athens seeing the sights. I'm sorry, it's going to take longer than I hoped. She's not due here for a week and a half."

"Are you just hanging around in paradise, killing time?"

"A little bit. I plan to spend time every day going through the company's books on my laptop and see if I can find a solution. Could you email me the last stocktake we did?"

"You should take time to enjoy the island."

Ella snorted. "Talking about enjoying the island...I went to the dig and met Liam's father."

"Crusty old professor?"

Ella wished Louise were right here with her. Seeing Aidan again had churned up so many emotions she didn't know how to feel. Louise had always been such a valuable touchstone of a friend, able to tell her when she was over the top, when she should step back and re-evaluate. They'd been that for each other—the keeper of each other's secrets.

"No. Not crusty. Not old, either." She wrinkled her nose. "In a crazy twist of fate, I know him. Liam's father is Aidan. My first boyfriend from Trinity."

Louise gasped. "The guy you flashed? You better start at the beginning."

Ella's mouth was dry by the time she finished telling Louise everything. Her friend agreed that it was better not to reveal to him that Amber and Liam wanted to get married.

"With all this extra time on my hands, I'll investigate some of the crafts on the island. There's gorgeous pottery everywhere, and I may find some interesting things for us to sell in *Precious Things*." With no salvation in sight for their shop, she still couldn't bear the thought of giving up on everything that she and Louise had built. "It's difficult to contact me on the island; coverage is spotty. If you send a text, I'll call you back when I get it, but that's the best we can do."

The call over, she checked the time—still early. Her help had been appreciated at the dig yesterday, and volunteering would serve to kill time before Amber's arrival.

She followed the same route as the day before and was

barely out of breath when she walked up to Betty, who was crouched working in the trench with Paolo.

"I didn't think you'd be back!" Betty's smile was wide and welcoming. "I'm delighted you are, though."

"I didn't know if your lost volunteers had turned up or not, so I decided to come and see."

Betty straightened, stuck out her hand, and Ella helped her out of the trench. "You can come every day?"

"For as long as I'm on the island, yes."

"Great. In that case, we need to do some paperwork." She strode toward the tent.

Aidan looked up when she entered. "Ella." He stood.

Betty explained that she needed Ella as a volunteer, then excused herself and returned to her trench.

Aidan rounded the desk. He stepped close and rested a hand on her shoulder. "I was obnoxious yesterday." Intense blue eyes stared into hers. "You left before I had a chance to say I'm sorry."

"Forget it. You were busy."

"Let me buy you dinner tonight to make up for it."

She nodded. Anything had to be better than sitting in her room with a thousand cats yowling outside.

"Good." He retrieved blank forms from the filing box under the table. "Name, address, telephone number, email...." He snatched a pen off the desk and handed it to her. "Fill this in. then sign at the bottom, and our insurance policy will cover you."

She did as he asked and handed the pages back. "Now you know everything about me."

"Hardly." His slow smile made a warm feeling unfurl in her chest. "We've been apart for a lifetime; we probably don't know each other at all." He put the pages into the filing box. "I'd like to know you now, as you are today."

"Me too." She wanted to touch him. Wanted to step close

and wrap her arms around his waist, as she had done so freely back then when they were in love. But he was right. Their history was just that, history.

He reached for her hand and turned it over, giving her palm all his attention. Ella held her breath. The dark sweep of his eyelashes hid his eyes. She was free to examine him thoroughly as he stared down. His skin was tanned by the Greek sun. His hair curled in that unruly way it did when it was a fraction too long, and her fingers itched to touch it. Everything about his face was so familiar and yet different. The jut of his cheekbones, the curve of his top lip, the dark shadow of scruff on his jawline, the strong column of his neck.

He stroked the exposed skin at her wrist.

In normal circumstances, Ella's swift intake of breath would have gone unnoticed. But these were not normal circumstances.

Aidan looked up, straight into her eyes. There was arousal in his eyes, matching the desire that coursed through her like a fast-flowing river. His thumb rested over her pulse point and time seemed to stop.

His gaze dropped to her mouth. She chewed her bottom lip, as was her habit when she was nervous, and shivered when he sighed.

Aidan released her hand and rubbed the nape of his neck. "I better let Betty have you." His shoulders tensed, and he took a step back.

* * *

Aidan was on his knees again. Typically, he took a supervisory role with the dig, but for the past week, he'd been more hands-on.

Ella wasn't trying to be seductive, but the lure of her presence tugged at his attention and fractured his focus. Since the day he felt her pulse accelerate beneath his fingers, he'd been tormented by a desire that hadn't bit so deep for years.

He couldn't and wouldn't act on it. Ella was here for one reason only, to meet her daughter. He wanted to kiss her, to touch her, to take her to bed. To give in to the attraction simmering under the surface of their every interaction, which was so strong it seemed that everyone noticed.

She was a member of his team. The mother of his son's girlfriend. If he could remember that, he could keep the boundaries in place between them.

Joining a volunteer in the trench every day, uncovering the next layer knee to knee, couldn't be criticized. Talking in hushed voices about everything in their lives while sharing a break under the olive tree could be brushed away as two old friends catching up.

But it was more. They both knew it.

She walked back to the village every afternoon, but apparently, she resisted siesta, preferring to catch up on emails and crunch spreadsheets in her room at the cat café. There seemed to be something going on with her business back in the States that she was reticent to talk about.

He'd taken her to the taverna next to the cat hotel for their first dinner. And it had become a habit to meet there every evening and share whatever the owner made for the evening meal. She always arrived first and claimed the table that had become theirs. Before her, a carafe of the local red wine waiting to be poured.

He felt a rush every time she noticed him in the doorway, and her face transformed with her smile. He'd been careful not to touch her again, but their days and evenings were more intimate than many of the nights he'd spent with others naked.

As long as he walked her to the door every night and didn't touch her, everything was under control, wasn't it?

Betty was on Ella's other side, and the two were engrossed

in conversation. He caught a fragment or two. Betty told Ella about the market that took place every Saturday and advised her to get there early. And then she invited Ella to join their little group for a Sunday hike in the mountains.

"Aidan."

He looked up to see Nick gesturing from the opening of the tent. He emptied the earth from his dustpan into the zambeli. He stood and brushed the dirt from his knees, then walked over.

"Let's take off early today." Nick gazed at the cloudless sky. "After the week we've had, we're due a break. I want to go surfing. You in?"

Aidan rolled his stiff shoulders. "I love that idea." His gaze wandered to the trench.

Ella's hair glinted in the sunshine.

"Bring Ella, if you want. She can lie on a towel and work on her tan."

Later that afternoon, Aidan and Nick sat on the beach swigging from bottles of beer as Ella surfed.

"I wouldn't have thought she was a surfer."

"She's pretty fearless." Aidan watched as she caught a wave and rode it to shore. "She lives in California, after all."

"She gave off a Mom vibe the first time I met her. Didn't she come to break up her daughter's relationship with Liam?" The corner of Nick's mouth curled.

Ella had been quiet since they arrived at the beach and had run straight into the water.

"That's not how she is." They hadn't been close for decades, and both of them had changed. But, the core of the woman she had always been remained the same. "She's just a little overprotective. It's not as though Liam and Amber want to get married or anything. They're both eighteen. I think Ella wants to make sure her daughter keeps focused on her studies and concentrates on passing her exams. They haven't been dating long."

Nick shrugged. He took a few moments to consider, then nodded. "I guess. Liam was crazy about Betty's daughter last year, wasn't he?"

"For a couple of months, yes. I don't know what it is about Liam that makes him fall so deeply. Maybe something about losing his mother...."

"You couldn't have done anything differently. I know he was just a teenager when Carol died, but the way your parents and sister helped means he had lots of support. I think Liam is just a romantic guy."

Aidan's family had rallied when Carol was diagnosed with cancer. His sister, Siobhan, had been an ever-present, hands-on auntie. She was two years older than him but hadn't married until five years ago. Now, while Aidan was paying university fees, she was chasing a couple of toddlers around.

Ella was riding a huge wave, wobbled, then was flipped off into the swell. Aidan stood and stared out at the waves until he saw her head appear. She waved in his direction, and he sat back down.

"So, you and her. What's happening?"

"I told you, nothing's happening. We were involved a long time ago, and it's good to see her again. Maybe things would be different if Amber and Liam weren't dating, but as it is, nothing's happening."

She ran out of the water dragging the surfboard. She readjusted her sensible black swimsuit and flicked back her long, wet hair. Her body was as good as it had been twenty years ago.

Nick laughed. "Keep telling yourself that."

Aidan shot him a glance.

"I've known you for years, man. And this is the first time I'm seen you fascinated. You can't keep your eyes off Ella, and you're defending her in conversation. You've already told me she was important to you once, and I'm reckoning she still is. This woman of yours has already surprised me by being a crazy-ass surfer. I thought she was a good girl, primary school teacher type, but now I'm getting bad girl, wild thing vibes."

"She keeps it hidden. Hell, she may not have followed her heart and lived on the wild side for years, but it's still there, deep inside."

"I'll keep an open mind." Nick grinned as Ella ran up the beach towards them.

* * *

On Saturday morning, Ella had a leisurely breakfast in the café and followed her usual routine of strolling to the circles to download her messages and emails. There was an email from Sandy quoting a price for *Precious Things*' building that made her eyes widen.

There was no way she could buy Jason out.

The news should have been depressing, but instead, her mood lifted as she paid for breakfast and picked up her jacket.

The narrowing of choices focused all the work she had been doing over the past week—all the thoughts she had about the future of her business, and a plan was forming.

The market was popular. The village square had been transformed by a mass of stalls piled high with all sorts of products. It seemed as though everyone bought fresh fruit and vegetables from the traders because villagers massed around the laden tables, testing, weighing, and measuring the produce for sale.

There were bottles of clear bottle-green olive oil, with sweet inky-black balsamic vinegar in squat corked containers stacked alongside. Ella bought a box of pastries topped with chopped nuts and honey and stowed it in her knapsack for later.

Food and drink stalls lined the left of the square. Ella wandered up and down, not buying anything except dried herbs and spices because she couldn't imagine packing them in her suitcase, and without a kitchen, there seemed little point in buying food.

The bustle of the stalls at the left dissipated somewhat as Ella turned the corner and changed direction to the array of stalls forming the back of the square. There were stalls with clothing, shoes, hats, and sunglasses. She picked up a pair of hiking boots and turned them over. A smiling woman in her fifties walked over to see if she could be of any help, and after an exchange part sign language, part semaphore found her the perfect size. And a chair so she could try them on.

Pleased with her purchase, Ella also bought a couple of long-sleeved shirts, some thick socks to wear with the boots, and a cap to keep the sun out of her eyes.

She walked on, then stopped in delight.

She'd always loved artisan crafts. The final side of the square showcased a treasure trove of beautiful things. There was stoneware pottery glazed in every shade of blue from sky to vibrant teal. Knitted sleeveless pullovers in featherlight gauzy wool piled high in a myriad of jewel colors. Semi-precious stones set in silver. Bowls of intricately fashioned silver rings. Beautiful supple leather handbags and luggage.

Ella let out a contented sigh. It was as though she'd died and gone to heaven.

A young man noticed her running her hand over all the wares on show and approached. "You like what you see?" His English was perfect.

"I love it. I love everything."

His wide answering smile lit up his face.

"Are all of the things made here on the island?"

He nodded. "Everyone makes different things."

"I'm Ella." Ella searched in her pocket for a business card and handed it over. "I own a small store in America, and I'd love to sell some of your things in my shop. Is there someone I can talk to about that?"

"Absolutely." The young man examined her card. "I am Sebastian. A few years ago, we formed a co-operative to make it easier to sell to buyers off-island. We don't have enough tourists without exporting."

His attention was caught by three women fingering some fine linen tablecloths hanging from smooth wooden poles to his left. "I'm sorry, I need to serve these ladies." He looked apologetic. "I'm on my own here for the next hour or so, and I cannot leave the stalls unattended. Would you like to come to our artisan center later today?" He scrawled down an address on a piece of paper and handed it over. "It is not far." He waved up the street and rattled off directions.

# Chapter Ten

The following morning, Ella was only a few steps away from the cat refuge when she encountered Aidan. He was dressed casually and carrying a white paper bag.

"I was just coming to find you." He held the bag aloft. "I brought pastries."

Ella's smile felt tight and forced. "Sorry, I have to be somewhere." She needed some time without him today. She'd bought tapas in the market yesterday morning and eaten them in her room last night rather than go to the taverna.

"Is there a problem?" His brow furrowed. "You didn't turn up last night—are you okay?"

"I'm fine." She gritted her teeth. Then she caught sight of her expression in a nearby window. Arms crossed. Teeth gritted. Plastic smile in place. The old Ella—the one who had been married to Jason. She'd reverted to the passive-aggressive ways she'd communicated with her ex-husband. There was a problem. She wasn't okay. Why not just tell him?

She uncrossed her arms and shook them out. "No. I'm not okay." She looked into his eyes. "I'm confused. We spent such a great day on Friday at the beach, but you acted strangely when we had dinner with Kitten. You hung on her every word and ignored me. It wasn't just me imagining it; both Kitten and Nick noticed. I was embarrassed."

He opened his mouth as if to refute her claims.

"I just don't know where we are or what you want from me. You're hot, and then you're cold. And the three of you walking me back to the cat rescue at nine o'clock and continuing on without me…." She breathed in. "It seemed rude."

"I'm sorry you feel that way." He didn't explain.

"Well, I have to go. I don't want to be late." She kept walking.

He walked next to her. "Where?"

She shot him an irritated glance. "I'm going on a hike."

Aidan shoved the bag of pastries into the pocket of his cotton jacket. "That sounds like fun. Can I tag along?"

"I guess so. We better hurry." The feeling of annoyance was challenging to maintain in light of his open, friendly manner.

They started walking toward the place she agreed to meet the others. The narrow road snaked out from the village up to the foothills of the mountain. Goats grazing on the verges ignored them entirely as they passed. Above, a small hawk hovered in the warm air, dark against the azure blue sky. Out here in nature, worries and concerns seemed to melt away. Ella concentrated on breathing in and out slowly, and felt her body relax.

Aidan cleared his throat. "I waited for you last night. Then I checked the cat rescue."

"You did?"

"I don't know if you were out or asleep, but I couldn't raise you. I tried throwing pebbles at your window and half expected you to appear on the balcony like Juliet. I guess once upon a time, I might have shinned up the trellis to catch your attention."

"I don't think the trellis could handle you."

He grinned. "I'm agile, but I'm not that agile. Not anymore."

The path twisted ahead. "Paolo said the cairns should be visible on our left after a sharp turn in the road," she said. "I'm guessing this is it."

"Ella!"

Paolo strode along the path to them. "Paolo!" She stepped forward and kissed the newcomer on both cheeks.

"Morning, Paolo." Aidan grinned. "I decided to tag along." He cast an eye between both of them. "If that's okay with both of you."

"It's not just us. Betty and Sharon are coming, too. Glad to have you along. It's better to have more men, yes?" He flashed a bright white smile in Ella's direction.

"Of course." She glanced down the road and spotted Betty and Sharon strolling in the sunshine. "It looks as though the rest of our party have arrived."

Once assembled, the group peeled away up a well-worn trail to the left, which snaked toward a rocky outcrop of large boulders. As they got closer, it became apparent that the path went straight through a gap between the massive stones.

"This is amazing." Ella flattened her palm against the warm stone then traced the striations in the rock's surface with her fingertips. "The way the stones are arranged—is it natural?"

"We don't think so." Betty walked through to the middle of a circle formed by the stones. "Not much research has been done about this site. But it appears as though the stones were placed to reflect the passage of the sun through the sky during the year. Much like Newgrange in Ireland and Stonehenge in

England, there's a tradition of people gathering here on special days to celebrate the changing of the seasons."

"There's a quarry on the other side of the island from where these rocks must originate. Dragging them here must have been a monumental task." Aidan climbed up onto one of the rocks furthest away from the center. He extended a hand. "I want to show you something. Come up here and see."

Ella placed her hand in his and climbed onto a narrow ledge next to him. There was little space. She had to lean against his body. One of his hands rested on her shoulder, and the other pointed out over the sea.

"You see that craggy rock in the distance? It's so small it couldn't have been inhabited, but there is a ruined stone outpost built on it which must have been used to signal if marauders were approaching. This island was under constant attack from the 12th Century onward by people on the other islands, pirates; you name it."

The moment before the other's arrival, when attraction hovered in the air between them like something alive, awakened an awareness that Aidan was finding hard to resist.

It was the same awareness that sprang to life on Friday, as they sat at the beach bar drinking mai tais and eating burgers. They'd shared a basket of fries, and he'd poured some onto his plate, and then hers. Normal, natural, the way anyone would. Anyone who is half of a couple. He'd looked up to see a knowing look on Kitten's face. As though she could see straight through him.

He'd put up a barrier to the intimacy building between him and Ella. Had focused on Kitten and Nick to divert feelings he didn't want to face. Despite Ella's presumption, he hadn't gone out drinking with the couple afterward. Instead, he had gone home early, alone.

Ella was brave enough to call him out on it. It was time for him to grow a pair and tell the truth.

The little group talked as they wandered through the ruins and continued around the headland. The wind whipped in from the sea, pressing against their faces and forcing their hair back from their foreheads. Aidan tried to shield Ella from the worst of it with his body, but she just laughed as the breeze flung her hair over her face and reached for his hand to steady her as she stumbled.

Was she even aware that she didn't let his hand go once they left the exposed coast behind and stepped into the cool forest?

He couldn't tell. She chatted with Betty as they crunched through the carpet of green needles underfoot. On the surface, it appeared as though she was giving the other woman all her attention, but her fingers still gripped his, and she edged closer, her hip brushing his. There was something electric, something clandestine about it. As though their bodies were talking to each other in a familiar language that only they knew.

He wished they were alone. If they were alone, he'd stop in the forest glade and tilt her face up to his.

She would give him her full attention.

He glanced at her profile, noting the pink flush of her cheeks, the soft curve of her mouth.

Ahead, Paolo stroked a strand of Sharon's blonde hair away from her face and tucked it behind her ear. He kissed her temple. The look she gave him in return was so filled with heat there was no way either of them would be spending siesta alone.

Ella's fingers curled around his tightly. She watched him with interest. "Okay?" Her voice was soft and knowing. He didn't want to label what he was feeling, but whatever it was, she felt it, too.

He wanted to kiss her. But now, in front of these people he worked with every day, wasn't the time or the place.

"Fine." He gently let go of Ella's hand and leaned forward to look across at Betty. "How much further is this place?"

"Another half an hour if we pick up the pace, an hour if we continue at a stroll."

"I vote we walk faster. I'm starving. Which way?" Ella stuffed her hands into her pockets and stepped ahead of Aidan, walking abreast with Betty. Within minutes they were deep in discussion about the archaeological site and the methods used in its excavation. Once Betty got into her stride, conversationally speaking, she could talk all day. She seemed to have concluded that Ella was a rank amateur she could educate.

Aidan had spoken endlessly about archeological processes when they were in college. He'd been a total bore about it. She even joined him for at least one weekend at the test pit he and another student dug at the bottom of his Uncle Eamonn's garden.

Ella seemed genuinely interested in what Betty had to say, though, occasionally responding with a pithy, relevant comment.

He followed. His gaze was drawn to the sparkling sea and azure sky. There was a little beach around here, tucked under the overhanging cliff and not visible from the path. He remembered visiting it once with Nick, tracking it down after they'd spotted it from a boat while fishing. Pale gold sand, sheltered by the curve of the headland from the wind. With tiny fish that swam around his ankles as he waded in the crystal-clear water. He'd love to take her there. If they were alone, he'd seek it out and take her there now.

But the little group marched on, paying little attention to

their surroundings—Betty's constant stream of conversation stifling the chance of a private discussion.

The sun blazed down on the top of his head. "Did you bring any water?"

Ella turned. "Yes." She stopped, and Betty did, too. After a second of rooting around in her bag, she pulled out a bottle and handed it over.

"Can I talk to you for a second, El?"

Betty glanced ahead, self-conscious. "I'll just..." Her lips wobbled into a smile. "Hold up, you two!" She walked fast to Paolo and Sharon.

"That was mean." Ella smiled. "You made her feel awkward."

"I just wanted to spend some time with you. Betty has a fear of silence; she always has to be talking, and she monopolized you for three-quarters of an hour. I got bored."

"You got bored." Ella strode along. "This is a hike. What did you expect?"

His laugh bubbled up from nowhere. "I guess I just remember a hike we went on. A long time ago."

Her eyebrows rose. "Oh, I remember." Her cheeks flushed pink. "That wasn't so much a hike as a hungover ramble. God knows whose idea it was, heading for the hills after the night we had. It was someone's birthday, wasn't it?"

"My cousin."

She nodded vigorously. "Your cousin." Her face contorted into a grimace. "Cheap Wine."

"Cheap vodka. And too much of it."

"I guess the idea was virtuous: heading out into the fresh air to clear our heads. And it got us away from the dozens of others with sore heads who'd slept over. But leaving the trail and finding that clearing in the woods with all the soft ferns—"

"Which were perfect for sitting on."

She nodded. "Perfect for sitting, and indeed for lying on."

The back of her hand swung close to his, close enough that if he rotated his wrist, he could catch her fingers. Awareness spun an invisible web between them as long-forgotten memories sprang to life.

His finger tracing the dip in her throat, continuing down her chest to the tiny white pearl button that fastened her red and white checked shirt closed. Her rose-colored lips parting a fraction as her cornflower-blue eyes watched every move he made. The hitch of her breath as he eased open the button. The vivid green of the ferns that surrounded her head like a vibrant living aura.

* * *

The restaurant was worth the hike. A small white building with a tiled roof faced the sea, with a terrace outside covered by a large pergola. The flowing vines that snaked up the heavy wooden timbers and scrambled over the top provided welcome shade to the diners seated at pale wooden tables beneath.

A pea-gravel circle was at the side of the building, with four or five cars parked inside.

"We could have driven up here?" Ella asked Betty.

"We could. But everything tastes so much better when you've worked for it." Betty walked ahead, striding down the little path to the doorway.

A wooden sign over the doorframe said Estiatorio Philoxenia. Minutes later, they were shown to a table and greeted by a smiling older man who introduced himself as Georgios, the owner.

He held an armful of menus but didn't hand them out. Instead, he explained how the restaurant's ethos was an ancient Greek one—to welcome and become friends to strangers.

"Philoxenia," he explained, waving to the sign above the door. "You are very welcome. Today is the first day we meet, but may it not be the last. All our fish and seafood is today's catch, and the herbs and vegetables are grown at my family's garden." He handed out the menus. "I will bring to the table a bottle of Robola from Kefalonia. It's a light, lemony wine. A present from me." He smiled, then departed.

Conversation flowed as the waiter brought food to the table. Fresh local fish, plump prawns, and glistening oysters. It all looked and tasted delicious.

Aidan and Paolo talked politics, Sharon and Betty discussed the recent excavated finds and what they hoped might still be discovered in the shallow trenches, and Ella leaned back in her chair and observed as she ate.

Added to the melody of the conversations were the light taps of knives and forks on porcelain. The clink of glasses against teeth. The peal of a woman at the adjoining table's warm laugh.

Ella leaned back in her chair. She was here, finally here, after so many years. In her twenties, she couldn't have imagined that two decades would go by before she left America again. The experience of being in a different country, immersed in a different culture, was exhilarating.

"How long are you here for, Ella?" Sharon asked.

"I'm not sure. A couple of weeks, maybe a little longer. You?"

There was a hint of sadness in Sharon's smile. "I'm here for another six weeks; then it's back to the UK to prepare for my last year at university." She glanced at Paolo.

"I'm here for four." Paolo reached for Sharon's hand and squeezed it. "Then I start my new job in Barcelona." His gaze met Sharon's and held. Neither spoke, but sadness shimmered in the air between them. Their newly blossoming relationship already had a time limit. Soon, they would be forced to part.

What point was there in starting a relationship under such tenuous circumstances? The closer they became, the more their inevitable parting would hurt.

Paolo held his glass aloft. "Live for today."

"For today." Sharon toasted too, as did Betty and Aidan.

Ella clinked her glass against the others' glasses in turn but couldn't bring herself to say the words. The magical sheen had worn off the day. Instead of being totally in the moment, she was plagued with harsh reality. She wasn't on vacation, or an enthusiastic volunteer at the dig, spending the summer with friends and sunshine. She was here for a purpose. To meet her daughter and stop her from making a foolish, ill-conceived marriage.

"Everything okay?" Aidan spoke low, concern evident in his tone.

"Yes, fine." She scrunched up the napkin in her lap. "Just returning to reality."

"This is real."

"Is it?" She'd spent the day holding hands and looking at Aidan through rose-colored glasses. Deluding herself that there was still something between them. Avoiding the fact that back home, her world was falling apart. "It's not my reality. I'm just a tourist. My real world is a disaster zone."

Aidan filled her glass. "Want to talk about it?"

Anxiety stiffened her shoulders and made Ella clench the napkin in her lap into a tight ball. Everyone was having a wonderful time. Voicing her problems in this setting would be an overshare.

"I don't...."

"Not here. Later. At my house. We can have a drink, chill out, and if you have any room left for food, I'll make us something."

They needed to talk in private and tonight seemed as good a time as any.

The waiter cleared their plates and placed a wooden platter of cheeses and figs into the center of the table.

Ella sipped her wine. "You're on."

# Chapter Eleven

Ella's clothes felt gritty with fine dust from the hike. The idea of a shower and a change of clothes before going out with Aidan was appealing, but first, she had her duties to deal with. Food and watering a houseful of cats, emptying litter boxes, and refilling them.

Just the thought of all the cat dander made her nose itch. She scratched it quickly, then slotted her key into the lock and pushed the door open.

Was there any news from back home? She checked her phone, but of course, there was no signal.

The first indication something was wrong was as she walked into the kitchenette where the cat feeding took place.

The bowls that she'd left down for the cats that morning now were washed and stacked on the draining board. A mop and bucket were in the corner, there was a lemony scent in the air, and the floor was spotlessly clean. The water bowls were full, and most of the cats seemed to have exited the cat flap for the day.

Someone had been in. There was nothing wrong with that —Elena told her a team of volunteers operated the cat rescue center. Naturally, they weren't going to alter their behavior just because she was staying there, but still, the thought that someone had been in the house while she was out made her uneasy.

There was no lock on the bedroom door. Believing she was alone, Ella hadn't taken any precautions to secure her belongings. When she woke, she'd stripped off her nightdress and underwear and left her discarded clothes where they fell before climbing into the shower. The thought that someone else—

Ella shivered. There was no point in stressing about it; the volunteer had saved her time. She should have anticipated the possible violation of her privacy. It wasn't something she could be angry about. Maybe she could get a key for the bedroom. Or lock her belongings into a cupboard or something.

She walked around downstairs, checking the litter boxes and noting that there were no jobs left for her to do. Then she climbed the stairs. She'd left the bedroom door closed, but it was now half-open. She took a deep breath and pushed the door wide.

Goldilocks and the three bears had been one of her favorite fairy tales as a kid. However, the reality that faced her was nothing like as appealing. A huge man, dark-haired and with a thick beard, sprawled asleep across the brass bed. His feet hung over the end, and his black boots were neatly lined up under the bed. Her white broderie Anglaise nightdress was on top of the pillow and under his swarthy head. God knows where her panties were. Two cats, who had joined the man for his nap, glanced over sleepily then continued their slumber.

She coughed. He slept on. She coughed again, louder. No response.

Ella clapped her hands together and stamped her feet. "Hello?" She cleared her throat. Took a deep breath, then shouted, "Hey!"

The stranger shot upright, eyes wide.

"What are you doing?"

He said something. By the lift of shoulders and simultaneous raising of eyebrows, it must be that he understood as much English as she did Greek—that's to say, none.

"I'm living here. This is my stuff." She waved at the bed. And pointed at her nightdress.

The nodding stranger climbed off the bed and scrabbled under the bed for his boots. He muttered words but didn't direct them at her.

"I guess you're a volunteer. I've seen that you've been looking after the cats." Ella forced herself to relax, to exude an understanding vibe. "I'm Ella." She tapped her chest. "Ella."

"Andreas." The giant held out a large hand. She shook it.

He backed away and turned around.

"Wait." Ella retrieved the pair of panties hanging off the back of his jacket, stuffed them hastily into her pocket, then waved him away.

Minutes later, the slam of the door telegraphed that Andreas had left. She watched from the balcony as he disappeared down the road and turned the corner.

The cats had followed Andreas from the room, so she closed the door before others breached the threshold. She turned the key in the lock and let out the breath she'd been holding. Everything here seemed different now. Her suitcase was open, her belongings scattered around the room she'd considered private. Andreas may have just come in for a sleep, but if curious, he could have looked through her things.

Ella felt sick.

It wasn't as though she had anything to hide, but the thought of a stranger breaching her privacy made her feel violated. There may be more than one other key to the sanctuary. If Andreas could let himself in, who else could?

There was no way she could stay here any longer. Not one

single night. There were still hours before she was due to meet up with Aidan, but she had plenty to do. She'd shower and then pack. In the next few hours, she must visit the hotel to hand back the keys and let them know she wouldn't be staying at the cat rescue center any longer. After that, she'd have a large glass of wine in the bar and call Louise.

She'd kept up a brave front in her other phone calls to Louise as her friend was dealing with enough problems. But emotions were heightened with Aidan and she needed her friend's dispassionate take on recent events. She was desperate to pour out all her feelings, tell Louise precisely what happened since she arrived on this godforsaken island, and if that meant standing in a painted circle while a café full of people watched and listened, so be it.

First though, a shower.

She pushed open the door to see the soap on the floor of the wet shower stall, and one of the fluffy white towels Kitten provided balled up on the floor. She stepped over it.

* * *

"Carafe or bottle?" Elena said in response to Ella's order of red wine. The right, responsible answer should be 'a glass.' There had been wine at lunch, and she planned on drinking later.

Her body was already betraying her mind when she was alone with Aidan. She didn't need any more factors thrown into the mix.

"Carafe, please, Elena."

"I'll put your bags behind the counter. Out of the way." Elena picked up Ella's suitcase and raincoat. "You're not leaving the island so soon?"

"No. Just moving."

Another group of people arrived at the table next to Ella's. With a glance and an apologetic smile, Elena excused herself.

Minutes later, she returned with a carafe of red wine, a glass, and a small plate with some olives and bread.

The first glass went down quickly. Ella was homeless, with no prospects in sight. Kitten had been sympathetic when Ella explained her afternoon's experience but had been unable to suggest a solution. There was still no room available in Twin Pines.

Ella poured more wine and sipped. The current plan was to throw herself at Aidan's mercy. He must have a sofa she could crash on until she could find something else. The weather was dry and warm; she could even camp out. Maybe he had a tent she could borrow. If not, she felt sure she could buy one somewhere in the village.

She chewed an olive.

It didn't look as though she'd have a chance to make that call to Louise this evening. Locals and tourists circled in and out of the white circles like bees visiting patches of flowers. As soon as one person finished their call and walked away, another stepped in and started to speak.

A guy at a nearby table made eye contact and smiled.

She glanced behind her. No one there. Oh. He's smiling at me. Ella smiled back, then glanced away, embarrassed.

"I'm not intruding, am I?" Aidan slipped onto the chair next to her. He glanced across at the guy she'd been flirting with, then looked into her eyes. "If you're busy, I can come back...."

She swatted him on the arm. "You want something to drink?" With a quick wave at a passing waiter and some short mime, she received an empty glass.

"Sure." He emptied the carafe into their glasses. "I was surprised to find your note."

She'd left a note pinned to the front door of the cat rescue center, asking him to meet her at the bar.

"Desperate for a drink." She swallowed a mouthful.

His eyebrows rose.

"I had a difficult day."

"A stroll and a delicious lunch? Here in Paradise?" He grinned. "Some people would call that okay. Not difficult."

"You think I'm entitled?" There was an edge to her words, even though they were packaged in a smile. When they were in college, he'd joked about the fact that she had everything handed to her on a silver platter. That she had not only been gifted her tuition fees and accommodation but had a healthy allowance which meant she always had the money for taxis after nights out.

While he had to work Saturdays and depended on his scholarship to pay his way.

"Well..."

"I used to be. I admit it. But this time, right now, I'm not. I'm stuck between a rock and a hard place, and with this Amber situation added to the mix...." She pressed her lips together and breathed in deep. "I'm struggling."

Aidan leaned forward. "What's happened?"

Ella blinked. "What do you mean?"

"You're so different from how you were earlier. You were tired but happy when we parted. Not looking forward to having this talk about Liam and Amber, but not stressed like you are now. What changed?"

"I don't have anywhere to stay any longer. Can I sleep on your sofa for a few days?"

He frowned. Nodded.

"Someone was sleeping on my bed when I got back. The stranger must have been another volunteer because he'd cleaned out the litter boxes, fed and watered the cats, and done all the other daily maintenance. He was probably exhausted."

"He was asleep on your bed?" Aidan crossed his arms.

"I don't feel comfortable staying there any longer. I'll move on as soon as I...."

"No, you won't. I have space; you're staying with me." Aidan swallowed the last mouthful of his wine. "Drink up. We need to go."

"Can we stay for a while? I want to call home." She pointed out at the white circles. "And this is the only place on the island I've found a signal." She rubbed the narrow stem of her wineglass between finger and thumb. "It looks as though everyone on the island has the same idea, though."

"I have cell phone coverage and internet at my house." Aidan stood and reached for her hand, pulling her to her feet.

"Your house is sounding more and more attractive by the minute." Her hand was still in his. She should let it go. But somehow, holding Aidan's hand felt natural. And he must feel the same way because he made no move to release her as they walked from the square further into the center of the town.

"I guess you haven't had much of a chance to explore." Aidan cast her a glance as they wove through narrow cobbled streets. The road rose before them. The shops and terraces were left behind, and before long, they were walking in nature. Ella noted windswept pines bent and twisted by the elements, scrubby undergrowth, and the tang of lemon in the air from a small plantation off the trail to their right.

"How far?"

Aidan released her hand and rubbed the back of his neck. He pointed ahead to a low white house with a tan terracotta roof behind old black iron gates. "We're here."

* * *

Aidan looked across the table at Ella. Before she arrived at the dig, he often ate here beside the swimming pool alone. He'd liked to light the candle in the middle of the table and watch the village below and the sea beyond.

Now, in her presence, the candle, the evening, the sparkle

of moonlight across the surface of the water, cast romance into the air.

"This is beautiful." She leaned back in her chair with a smile curving her lips. "And dinner was great."

Aidan shrugged. It was difficult to mess up a one-pot meal.

Ella sipped her wine. She seemed calm and content as she gazed out into the soft darkness. He'd held her hand once more when they left the taverna. And, despite himself, he had been unable to let it go. He was caught in a memory of how they always held hands as they walked around Trinity. And when they reconnected at the end of the day, they were inextricably drawn together like magnets. They held hands all the time. She was the only person he'd ever done that with. Carol hadn't been tactile in that way, and he—well, somehow, he just never reached for anyone's hand in the way that he had Ella's.

He hadn't even realized their hands still connected them until he made eye contact with one of the locals as they walked through the village and had noticed the stranger's gaze dip to their clasped fingers and then back up to his eyes with a smile. A knowing smile. An 'oh, you're in love' smile.

Another one of those wake-up call smiles.

"We need to talk about Friday." He topped up both of their glasses. "You were right. I ignored you."

Ella frowned. "Why?"

He swallowed the rest of his wine. It might be time to open another bottle. He stood. "I think we need more wine. I'll get some."

He stalked around the kitchen, locating a bottle of red, opening it, and then bracing his hands on the metal draining board to look out into the dark night. Once he told her how he felt, it would be over, and the knowledge chewed him up inside.

"Aidan?" Ella's voice was soft.

He turned to see her hesitate in the doorway, looking at his face as if judging his mood from his eyes and his facial expression.

He should lock his emotions away. Should plaster on a carefree smile, and take the bottle of wine outside. Not do what his body wanted and take her to bed.

She stepped forward, and all his intentions of keeping her at a distance dissolved.

Before she could utter another word, he swept his arms around her and claimed her mouth in a kiss.

# Chapter Twelve

*Aidan is kissing me.*

In a haze of sensation, Ella's mind registered that not only was Aidan kissing her, but also that she was kissing him back, without restraint. She'd always loved the way he kissed her. The way the world seemed to slip away, and nothing else mattered when their mouths met. She was incapable of rational thought. It wasn't possible to do anything but enjoy the sensations flooding her body at his touch.

*What are you doing?*

The voice in her head grew louder, shouting to get her attention.

She jerked back and gazed up into his midnight blue eyes. "Aidan." Her voice sounded shaky and unsure. She swallowed, then tried again. "Aidan, what are we doing?"

"You know what we're doing, Ella." His mouth curved into an intimate smile. The secret 'you and me' smile she hadn't seen for decades but recognized instantly. He looked the way he always looked when they were in their own private world, communicating one to one—soul to soul.

She did. She also knew if neither of them slammed on the brakes, they'd be naked in each other's arms tonight.

She took a step back. Aidan's arms fell to his sides. "We should talk about this."

"And say what? It's just a kiss. It doesn't warrant an in-depth conversation."

"Just a kiss?" Her insides had melted at the mere touch of his lips on hers. She'd been ready to throw caution to the wind and get swept away in a tsunami of passion. In her mind, she'd gone all the way, imagining them in bed together. Wondering how his body had changed, hoping he wouldn't judge the changes in her body too harshly. She wasn't a twenty-something anymore. She was a forty-year-old with silvery stretch marks.

"Just a kiss." He snaked an arm around her waist. Then he pulled her close. "Just lips. Touching." He leaned close. His warm breath feathered against her lips as he whispered: "Nothing more."

The choice was hers to make. Tilt her mouth to Aidan's, or let the moment pass. If she let the moment pass, they would continue back the way they had before she walked into the kitchen. They would take that bottle of wine outside and talk about the dilemma of their children's future like the sensible adults they were. She wouldn't have to explain that she thought kissing him was a bad idea; wouldn't have to open up the Pandora's box of their past.

But if she didn't kiss him at this moment, it would be over.

She wasn't ready for it to be over. With a sigh, Ella slid her hands up Aidan's chest. She stroked his tense shoulder muscles, then linked her hands behind his neck and pulled his mouth down to hers.

Just a kiss? Not by any stretch of the imagination could 'just a kiss' describe the conflagration that blazed through her the moment their lips met. His hands were at her waist, at her back, ranging all over her body, compelling her closer. Her fingers speared through his hair.

She was in the fevered grip of a passion she couldn't remember feeling for years. The feel of his lips on hers, the taste of his mouth, the curling spring of his hair beneath her fingertips, all combined into an intoxicating, irresistible experience.

He broke the kiss to nuzzle the side of her neck. She angled her chin up, allowing him better access, and groaned aloud.

"God, that's good."

In response, his hands slipped under the hem of her tee-shirt and clasped her sides. She'd always loved the way he did that. The way he held both sides of her waist as though she was his. As though he'd never let her go.

He'd been her first everything. First crush. First kiss. First lover.

She'd been his first, too.

Jason had been her second. Right now, in the silent kitchen, it was as if there had been no one else for either of them since they were last together.

Aidan's moves were smoother. When he lifted her onto the wooden kitchen table, it was without pausing or taking a breath. He'd always driven her wild, but now there was no hesitation in the way he peeled off her tee-shirt and unfastened her bra.

With him, she'd been brave, been bold, been Trouble.

And that old feeling of complete confidence and safety with him welled to life as she unfastened each button of his shirt, then shoved it from his shoulders.

Reckless. Wild. Wanting.

She pressed her lips to his collarbone. Smiled against his skin at his swift intake of breath. Heard him whisper, "Trouble," before she kissed up his neck to his warm, waiting mouth.

There was something perfect about coming together. Something timeless. Ella had assumed her libido had gone into retirement as a by-product of being older. Her marriage had cooled years before they called time on it, and she'd resigned herself to never feeling these feelings again.

Aidan's hands went to the button of her jeans. She hadn't had sex in months, and even then, it had been a hurried affair under the covers in a dark bedroom. Were they really about to have sex on a kitchen table? Could she even take her jeans off without falling onto the floor?

A laugh bubbled up from somewhere.

Aidan's hands stilled. He tipped up her chin and examined her face. "Is this okay?"

"I'm just laughing at the idea of falling off this table. I'm not as limber as I once was." She grinned.

"You look the same as you did when you were twenty." He stroked a hand over one of her breasts. "Just as beautiful."

Her heart pounded. Everything was way out of control. She wasn't just about to have wild, crazy sex with this man; she was about to tumble back in love with him again. And, heaven help her, there didn't seem to be anything she could do to hold herself back from the brink.

"But the last thing you need is a broken leg." There was a wicked warmth in his smile. "So how about you slip off that table, and we take this to the couch?"

* * *

There were so many chances to change course. While they were kissing, Aidan had been caught up in the moment. He'd wanted nothing more than to keep kissing, keep touching. But once she broke the spell by laughing about falling off the table, things took a different turn.

The heat changed from an out-of-control blaze to a slow,

steady burn. A mystical moment had captured he and Ella in its spell. Either of them could call a halt, but neither seemed able to. Getting involved with Ella would mean trouble for both of them. But it was as though Aidan consulted one of those old maps with 'here be monsters' written in the middle of uncharted seas and set sail straight for them anyway.

"Come on."

She grabbed her clothes and pressed them to her chest. Grinned up at him as if acknowledging that what they were doing was crazy, totally crazy, but she was in it just as much as he was.

The urge to kiss her again was overwhelming. What would have been the point in resisting anyway? They were both adults and not hurting anyone. They kissed as they walked. Both clumsily lurching from room to room until they reached the long sofa. Bulky removable cushions covered the wicker framework. On previous stays on the island, they had been taken off and laid on the ground to form a makeshift bed.

Aidan sank onto the sofa and felt the hard presence of his cellphone in his back pocket. "Hang on." He retrieved it and placed it on the coffee table.

"You done?" A sensuous smile curved Ella's lips.

"All done." He couldn't look away. She was luminous. Compelling.

Without breaking his gaze, Ella let her hands fall to her sides. The clothes she carried tumbled to the ground. "Kiss me."

A shadow memory of how they used to be, how it was when she was in his arms bled through him like muscle memory as he leaned in to claim her full lips. He closed his eyes and breathed in her scent, recognized her taste, and when her shoulder lifted a fraction, he remembered how she'd always been so responsive when his fingers skimmed there.

Being with her was beguiling, like returning to a place

visited in childhood. Or like rewatching a much-loved movie he hadn't seen for decades. Familiar, yet different. Her soft breasts pressed against his bare chest as they got closer—so close there was nothing between them. His body ached with a desperate need, but this—just kissing her and feeling her body beneath him—was so delicious Aidan wouldn't hurry.

Her fingers speared through his air, massaging his scalp. She moaned softly, and heat blazed through him in a flash.

A few times over the years, he'd thought about them together. They'd explored each other's bodies with wonder and delight. She was the first woman who saw him naked—the first he'd brought to orgasm. People always said you never forget your first time, and it had been impossible to forget Ella, much as he might have desired to.

No woman had ever affected him as she did. He'd written it down to youth, inexperience, and rose-tinted memories, but now?

Now it was as if the door to the past had opened, and he walked straight through it holding her hand. His tongue traced her lips, then plunged inside. She groaned, and his cock pressed hard against his jeans in response. He cupped the back of her head and her neck angled to follow the movement of his mouth.

"You still love her, don't you?" The long-forgotten question whispered in his mind. Carol had asked him on their third date about his ex-girlfriend, the one other students had not been able to stop talking about.

From those who hadn't been there, the story was that she'd flashed a lecturer and been expelled. That she'd always been known as Trouble and had lived up to her nickname. The gossip continued that she dumped Aidan without even a word, leaving him shattered and heartbroken.

It was common knowledge that he didn't even want to hear her name. Friends started referring to her as 'the one that got away' instead. When Carol asked the question on their date, to Aidan's annoyance, a mental picture of Ella appeared into his mind; grinning as she pulled up her tee-shirt to flash him her boobs, not noticing the lecturer walking up behind him in the darkness.

"I don't love her. I don't even like her." He'd pushed memories and hurt feelings aside and forced himself not to think of her. She'd hurt. She was Trouble. She left without a word or a way to contact her, and whatever they once had was now firmly in the past.

"Aidan," the woman under him whispered. Her hands caressed his waist.

What the hell am I doing?

He pulled away. Sat up and faced away. With the back of his hand, he wiped her taste from his lips. His heart hammered fit to burst.

She placed her hand on his naked back. He flinched, and it fell away.

"What's the matter? Aidan?"

"We shouldn't do this." He rubbed a hand wearily through his hair. "This is wrong. For a whole heap of reasons."

"You mean Amber and Liam?" She struggled vertical and swung her legs out to sit next to him on the sofa. "I know. I don't know how on earth we'll explain our relationship if they get married. I guess the fact that we dated before—"

His head twisted to her. "We're not a couple. We're not going to become a couple. I gave you my heart once, Ella; I won't again."

Her cheeks flushed pink, and she looked down, avoiding his gaze. "I didn't mean—"

"The most this would be for either of us is a hook-up. A hot and heavy stroll down memory lane. We wouldn't be confessing to our kids." His words were harsh, brutally honest. He had to deny her effect on him for his own preservation. With her so close, he had lost objectivity. He was vulnerable.

Ella wrapped one hand around her chest. She searched the carpet for her discarded clothing.

He picked up her clothes and handed them over.

"Let's just forget this ever happened." Her voice was even and measured. "It won't happen again."

* * *

Remaining in the same room as Aidan after his rejection was impossible. Ella got out of there as quickly as she could.

She lay in the dark for hours, listening to the muted sounds of him moving around downstairs. What had happened? They'd both seemed to be on the same page, had been moving inexorably closer to the moment they'd be having sex, but then something happened. He stilled and pulled away.

"I gave you my heart once, Ella; I won't again."

If anyone should be mistrustful, it should be her. Aidan had made no effort to contact her after she left Ireland so many years ago. Who said what was between them involved their hearts anyway?

She shivered. She wasn't ready to fall in love and hadn't even considered that their coming together would be anything but a stolen moment. So why did her heart ache? Why did it seem as though something precious and vital, once lost, had been rediscovered then cruelly snatched away?

She tossed and turned in bed, unable to get comfortable.

Aidan had gone to bed hours ago. The light that spilled out from the sitting room had gone dark, and then she heard his footsteps on the stairs and the creak of the bedroom door opposite opening and closing.

She threw off the light coverlet and walked in the dim

moonlight to the open window. The night was so still no breeze lifted the lace curtains. She stared out over the darkened garden and trailed her fingers across the bottom of the window frame.

Everything here was different. Even the air smelled different, warm, dry, and fragrant with the scent of rosemary and thyme that must grow in the bed under the window.

In such a short time, her everyday reality had faded away. She'd lost track of who she was, where she was. Had somehow traveled back in time to the days when Aidan was more important to her than anything else. It was a totally false reality. She needed to become grounded; she must shift her focus from fantasy to real life.

Aidan said there was a phone signal in the house.

She'd left her phone downstairs in her bag. Ella pulled on her cotton dressing gown and went downstairs.

Twenty-seven texts.

Ella blinked. Twenty of them from Louise. And voicemails. Lots of voicemails. There were a couple of texts from Amber, too.

She sat on the sofa in the darkness and placed a call. Louise answered immediately. "Where the hell have you been? I've been worried sick!"

It wasn't like Louise to be so upset. She was constantly berating Ella for being over-protective of Amber and was now acting in the same manner. "What's the matter?"

"Things are crazy here. I don't know where to begin." Louise paused. "I don't know where to start."

"Just relax."

"Relax! Hang on a second. I'm getting a drink."

Ella tucked her legs up under her on the sofa.

"We had a water leak at *Precious Things*."

"Oh no." Her chest tightened.

"It brought down a portion of the ceiling. I opened up

your beach house and diverted the deliveries we had outstanding—Susan Whitmore's sofa, the lamps for Barney, the oriental rugs for Conrad Jackson—"

"Oh, god."

"Oh god is right. We've spent the past few hours salvaging what we can, but the water destroyed a lot. There was no room in your house for the furniture items, so I had to make other arrangements."

"Of course. What did you do?"

"I asked around, and Alison recommended a storage facility, so I hired a unit there. I've used movers to clear the space, and we're stowing whatever we can at the storage unit. It's not ideal, but at least it's safe."

"Good thinking. You've paid from the company account?"

"Yes."

"Okay, so I need to call the insurance company." She grabbed a notebook and a pen from her bag.

"I looked through the filing cabinet, found their number, and called them. The assessor is due in a couple of days."

"What else?" Ella's brain was fried with this new situation. Sandy was waiting for her to commit to selling the premises, but the leak meant work would need to be done. "A plumber? A builder?"

"A plumber has already been, and he is replacing some pipes which had corroded. I knew you'd want me to sanction that, and I've paid out of the company account."

"Good, good." Ella nodded. "I'll need to find a builder." She jotted it down on her piece of paper. "Thank you so much for dealing with all of this. Amber is due here in a couple of days, but I'll have to move that up. I need to be home sorting all these problems. I'll call her now."

Louise sighed. "Amber rang. She told me she's been trying to get in contact, and you haven't replied. She said you'd always been contactable, and when you weren't, she was worried something might have happened to you."

"What did you say?"

"The first time, I told her you weren't in today, and maybe your phone was out of charge. But when I couldn't get in contact, and she called back, I had to tell her you went to Greece."

"Oh." Ella chewed on her bottom lip. "When did you talk to her?"

"Yesterday morning. She knows you're on Kosmima. I wish you had better cell phone coverage. Are you at the circle again?"

"No. I moved in with Aidan. It's a long story. I'll call her."

"I wouldn't be surprised if she's already on her way to confront you. She was mad. She kept saying she couldn't believe that you would fly to Greece on your own to try and mess with her life. Her words, not mine."

# Chapter Thirteen

It should have been easy to sleep. But the encounter with Ella left Aidan wired and restless. He'd heard her door creak open in the middle of the night. And for a moment, he considered following her back into the sitting room to talk—to explain how being so close to her tangled his emotions making him act in a way he couldn't recognize, never mind control.

He even swung his legs out of bed and reached for his jeans. But then he heard her talking low and quietly in the sitting room. She must have decided to make the call she said she wanted to earlier in the evening. Aidan dropped his jeans on the floor and lay back in bed, putting his arms behind his head as he stared up at the ceiling.

She'd always had the ability to tie him up in knots. To make him talk when he didn't want to, and act from the heart rather than his head. One of his strongest memories was of them on a warm night like tonight, dancing barefoot in the grass at a friend's twenty-first birthday party. James Taylor's voice drifted in the air from a large white marquee their friend's parents had hired for the event. Inside, drinking games were taking place, and the crowd was becoming loud and rowdy. Outside, on the lawn a distance away, they danced. Nothing mattered except the feel of her body against his, the warmth of her hand on his shoulder, and the way their bodies swayed together.

She'd spoken of never wanting to go back to America again.

He breathed in her scent and wished they could stay this way forever.

"Aidan?"

Aidan opened his eyes. The woman in his dream was in his room, hovering over the bed. She wore an oversized tee-shirt which revealed a flash of white panties.

Her hair was mussed and wild. Her eyes wide and panicked. She held out Aidan's cellphone. "I put it on mute. It's Liam. I answered it." She looked as though she might cry. "I'm sorry, I was asleep on the sofa, and it rang on the coffee table. I thought it was mine. I didn't mean to...."

"Fine." He shifted up in bed and rearranged a pillow over his lap to hide his morning wood.

She was still standing there, looking at him. "Go make coffee or something." He took the cellphone.

"I should, um—"

He waved her off and fiddled with the phone. "Liam!"

"Dad."

There was a world of words unsaid in Liam's tone. Maybe he could steer the conversation away from the inevitable.

"So, how are you both? Coming to Kosmima soon?"

There was silence down the line for an uncomfortable couple of minutes. Then, just when Aidan thought he'd got away with it: "Dad. An American woman answered your phone, and Amber says her mother is in Greece. What the hell's going on?"

There was a noise from the kitchen. A door slam, the

banging of pans, then the unmistakable crash of something pottery hitting the terracotta tile floor followed by a loud "Fuck!"

Exactly.

"Amber's mother, Ella, is staying here."

Liam didn't respond. The silence stretched until Aidan couldn't bear it any longer. "She turned up here looking for you both. I didn't call you because she wanted to surprise Amber."

"So a complete stranger tracked you down and asked for a bed? I'm sorry, Dad. Amber says her mother is hard work, but I didn't expect she'd go this far."

Aidan frowned. "It's not like that. She didn't ask me for a bed, but the place she was staying was unsuitable. And Ella isn't hard work."

"You don't know her. Amber says she's a helicopter mother; she can't help hovering." Liam laughed. "Her father is cool, though. He's very easygoing."

Despite himself, Aidan found himself standing up for his long-ago ex. "She's just concerned." He took a deep breath. Now that the truth was out that Ella was staying in his house, he couldn't keep their previous relationship secret. "And, funny thing...Ella and I know each other. Well, we knew each other. Back in the old days. In Trinity."

Carol had always joked about catching him on the rebound. Even though she never met Ella, their love story had been common gossip in the months after Ella left. He'd been identified as the one left behind and her as the one that got away. Years later, Carol joked about the one that got away with more than a touch of jealousy behind her joking.

"Wait." Liam let out a shocked gasp. "American. In college with you at the same time. Oh my god, you're not telling me that Ella is the one that got away?"

Oh boy. Life just got complicated. "It was a long time ago."

"I have to talk to Amber." His voice lowered to a hoarse whisper. "She wasn't in bed with you when I called, was she? For god's sake, Dad, keep your pants on."

"Go talk to your girlfriend." Aidan kicked off the covers and swung his legs out of bed. "I need coffee."

"I can't believe Ella flew across the world to break the news to you even though she knew Amber and I were coming here to tell you face to face."

Aidan rubbed a hand over his face. He bent down to grab his shoes from under the bed. "What news?"

"That we're engaged. That we're going to be married before Christmas."

Aidan gritted his teeth. "I'll call you back."

* * *

"Hey."

Ella straightened at his welcome. She carried a dustpan full of shards of broken pottery. "I smashed a bowl. Sorry."

Aidan shrugged. "I heard it drop."

She slid the shards into the bin and gestured to the stove. "There's coffee in the pot."

"We're going to need it." He poured a cup and refilled hers. "That didn't go so well."

"Tell me about it. I swear everything's gone wrong in the past twenty-four hours. There's been a water leak at my business, and trying to help at a distance in different time zones is a nightmare." She had dark circles under her eyes. "I need to be home, not here.

She pushed back the cloud of golden hair from her face and tugged at the hem of the tee-shirt. It would be easier to concentrate if she put some clothes on.

He must have been staring because she flushed pink and sank onto the sofa, tossing the throw over her legs.

"Well, Amber now knows you're at my house."

She grimaced.

"Liam was under the impression that you came to the island to tell me he was getting married. He was angry. I don't understand why you didn't tell me."

She ran her hands through her messy hair. "I couldn't. Amber told me Liam was coming to the island to tell you about their plans in person, and I didn't want to spoil that moment for him. Although I was hoping you'd think they were too young to rush into marriage. Unlike my idiot ex-husband, who gave them his blessing without reservation."

"I accused you of being overprotective. I wouldn't have been so judgmental if I'd known the true situation."

She blew out a breath. "They're eighteen in their first year of college. Amber's considering dropping out and getting a job. With no qualifications, she'll only find minimum wage. And she'll be forced out of college accommodation. I don't have any problem with their relationship; I came to talk them out of a wedding."

"For what it's worth, I agree. Liam has a lot of work to do, and he lives at home with me."

"I'm sorry I didn't tell you. I wanted to so many times." She stared down at her hands. "We'll have a lot of talking to do when they turn up."

It was impossible to stay angry at her. Aidan might have done the same in her place. But she was right. The next few days would be difficult. "I had to tell him that we...uh... weren't strangers."

Her eyes widened. "Liam knows about us in college?" Her voice rose in panic. "Oh no." This was so much worse than she'd imagined. "I've never told Amber about the *disgraceful incident*."

"The *disgraceful incident*? There was nothing disgraceful about you flashing your boobs at me across the quad. You were so impulsive, so fun, such Trouble." He lowered his brows and said the last word in his deepest voice and felt an unexpected rush of joy when the corners of her mouth turned up in a smile, and she laughed in response.

"That's the first time in years I've thought of that moment with an emotion other than shame." Her smile faded. She rubbed her eyes. "My parents hammered into me that the way I behaved had been worse than unbecoming. My mother used the word slutty, and my father was so disappointed he couldn't look me in the eye. "

She grimaced. "I wish I'd realized a member of staff was walking up behind you. I would never have done it if I'd known someone other than you would be receiving an eyeful." She scrunched up her eyes and rubbed them with her fingertips. "Being reported for lewd conduct and exposing myself was too shameful for my family to deal with. I knew my parents were flying in to speak to the dean that morning—the last morning I saw you."

"You didn't say anything." She hadn't. He would have remembered.

"No. I didn't. I knew if I did, you'd stay to meet my parents and would defend me. I didn't want that. I thought I could handle the situation better on my own. That I could talk my parents around, that they'd chastise me, and that would be it. The college had given me a warning and suspended me for a couple of weeks. I was more than ready to accept my parents' censure."

She stared out of the tent to the bright sunlight beyond.

"It didn't work that way. They withdrew me from university and put me on the next plane without consultation, and refused to listen to any of my appeals. I managed to slip a note to a girl to pass on to you—she said she knew who you were, but she wasn't one of our regular gang. I couldn't pass it to any of our mutual friends. They were all in class, and my parents wouldn't let me say goodbye."

Their breakup had scarred him for years. He buried his feelings rather than confronting them. The aftermath of Ella's callous abandonment hardened his heart. Their history made her impossible to trust.

Was she telling the truth?

"I never got a note."

Her eyes widened in a surprise she couldn't hide. "You didn't?"

He shook his head. "One minute you were there, the next you were gone. I tried calling you, but I could never get through."

Ella's face crumpled. "I let my parents put me on that plane. They insisted on taking my phone. I thought you'd write to me when you couldn't reach me. But when I didn't hear anything, I gave up. I was in love with you, but I thought maybe you didn't feel the same. That you'd moved on."

Everything he thought he knew about Ella's life shifted.

He moved from the chair to sit beside her on the sofa. "The *disgraceful incident* was the way they behaved." He placed his hand over hers. "My memory of that night is diamond clear. I remember everything about it. The way you looked at me as though there was no one in the world apart from you and me. Your secret smile. The grin when you lifted your shirt. Sure, other stuff came after, but that moment...."

"You're smiling." She brushed her fingertips across his lips.

"So are you. It's a good memory."

"Yes, it is. Thanks for reminding me." She looked at his mouth, and in a flash, he was right back there, at that moment when the rest of the world fell away, and there was nothing but the two of them.

"Well." He shifted away from her and reclaimed his coffee

cup. “I think I need some more coffee. I just want to run away from this situation—I bet you do too.”

She frowned. “I thought you understood I didn’t have any choice about leaving. I didn’t run away by choice. I was taken.”

“I don’t mean that. I remember you always talked about getting out there and seeing the world. We dreamed of Venice in February, Paris in springtime, camel rides in Egypt, all that stuff.” He cast her a glance. “You got to do at least some of that, right? You said your parents were strict, but once you finished college, you traveled?” Her open-eyed zest for life, for new experiences, had been such a large part of who she was he couldn’t imagine she hadn’t followed her heart.

Ella’s mouth turned down at the corners. She rotated the mug in her hands and looked at the coffee table rather than at him. “I didn’t get the chance to enroll in college in the States. My parents took the position that my behavior showed I wasn’t college material, so I started working for a friend of my father’s in a clothing store. I met Jason and married young. Had Amber.” Her eyes finally met his. “I don’t regret a moment of it. She’s a blessing. A wonderful girl.”

“Carol was pregnant with Liam when we got married. Life doesn’t always work out the way we plan.”

“Life isn’t over yet.” Ella’s chin tilted up, and a flash of Trouble made itself known. “Now that I’m divorced, and Ella doesn’t need me so much, I plan to chase down some of those things on my bucket list.”

“I skydived.” That had been on her list.

“You did?” Her eyes rounded in wonder. “Was it as wonderful as we thought it would be?”

“I was fine until they opened the door of the Cessna, then I was shit scared. It was terrible. I tried to wriggle out of it.”

“You did not.” Her grin was wide, imagining.

“I did. I offered the instructor a bribe to let me sit it out. It was one of the most mortifying experiences of my life. The other skydivers, kids, housewives, even a guy in his eighties, were scornful. But what could I do?" Embellishing the story just to amuse her was fun.

"Let me guess, at the last minute, the instructor pushed you out?"

For a brief moment, fear gripped his insides, but then he'd been filled with excitement at the prospect of hurtling into the blue. "He peeled my fingers off the side of the door."

Her loud and genuine laughter rang out, and before he knew it, he was laughing right along with her.

"Peeling your fingers off the door," she managed between laughs.

"With one hand, while the other pushed me out."

"He should have tickled you." Their gazes met. "That would have made you let go."

"You remember."

She hadn't tickled him often because it always ended up with him retaliating and tickling her back. They always ended up in each other's arms afterward.

"I remember everything."

* * *

It was happening again. Ella was falling back into the strange state she found herself in sporadically since reconnecting with Aidan. A condition where the emotions of the past were in danger of overwhelming the woman she was now. She'd never been at risk of succumbing to magic with Jason; their relationship had been based on solid things like bringing up a child, running a house, supporting each other in their endeavors, his work, her shop.

Being with Aidan blurred the lines of past and present. She didn't feel her age, didn't feel staid and stale any longer.

Life was there, ready for the taking, ready to be embraced. Back home, while sorting out her old papers, it felt as though the person she'd been was a stranger. She'd thought, *Where did that girl go*?

Now, the presence of her old self infused every atom. She'd always been present, just repressed. Out of sight, out of mind.

If only she could stop thinking about kissing him.

She wasn't even aware she was staring at Aidan's mouth until he leaned close. She'd been here before, and the last time he pulled away. The prospect of being rejected again stopped her from pressing her lips against his.

She shifted, and the blanket slid from her knees to the floor.

Aidan reached for it but missed. His hand brushed against her body, and she shivered in response.

With a slow slide, his hand progressed from knee to thigh. The kiss started gentle and deliberate, then caught fire. Ella's fingers speared through his hair, twisting a curl between her fingertips. Her knee lifted, and his hand curled around and stroked the sensitive skin behind her kneecap.

There was nothing else in the world but the two of them.

Aidan's hand moved to her throat. To the curve of her neck.

"I have to go to work," he murmured against her mouth. "I don't want to go to work."

"Snow day?" A smile curved her lips.

He groaned. "I can't. We're having a meeting at ten." He traced the small, curved bones at the bottom of her neck with his fingertips. "I can be back for lunch, though."

"We could have a picnic in bed."

"Good idea." He kissed along her jawline. Then reluctantly shifted away and stood. "I'll shower, and then go." His gaze rested on her, and the heat in his eyes' depths filled her with warmth. "I won't invite you to join me because then I'd never leave."

Arousal made her body languid. "I should call Amber."

Aidan took a step away, then another. He walked backward, watching her face every step until he had no option but to turn and walk from the room.

Ella reached for her phone. "Hi, Amber."

There was silence on the other end of the phone for a moment. Then the slight hitch of Amber taking in a deep breath, fueling herself for a tirade.

"I cannot believe you came to Greece to turn Liam's father against him. How could you, Mom? How could you act as though you were happy for me and then try to break us up?"

"That's not what happened. I came to Kosmima to see you and to meet Liam. And I hadn't told Aidan anything. He had no idea about the marriage plans until Liam dropped that on him this morning."

"What?" She sounded stunned.

"Didn't Aidan tell Liam he had no clue you were engaged?"

"I don't think so. Liam was ranting about you spoiling the surprise. He can't possibly know that you didn't tell. So, what have you been doing on the island by yourself? Liam said you know his dad and told me some story about you stripping in public. I don't understand what's going on."

"I'll explain it when I see you." Life was too short to try and explain the *disgraceful incident* to her daughter over a patchy phone connection. "The important thing is that I'm fine. Aidan and I have been catching up and spending some time together, and I'd like to see you as soon as possible. There's a problem with the store. I'm sure Louise told you, so I have to cut my trip short and go back home to sort everything out."

"Can I come, too?" Amber's voice was quiet. There was a

hint of sadness in her voice. "I think I need to go home and think about things."

Ella was instantly in defensive mode. "What's the matter? Is everything okay between you and Liam?"

She'd come to the island to stop Amber from making a mistake, but she didn't wish her unhappiness.

"He wants to sail to the island. I've told him how I get seasick, but he keeps telling me I'll love sailing from island to island. We met a guy two days ago who asked Liam to crew. He's so excited to do it, but I'm afraid I'll be seasick, and the experience will be ruined for everyone on board as a result."

"I suppose the other alternative would be the ferry. Maybe you could come on the ferry."

"He sails with a gang of beautiful rich kids, and I come on the ferry?" She sounded scathing. "I don't see how that's supportive of him. I told him I was less likely to be vomiting if I was on the ferry, but he says I should take a chance and try the yacht. I think I should come on the ferry and he should, too. For solidarity. Because if I'm going to be his wife, he should back me up in stuff like this."

"Talk to him. Maybe you could take some seasick pills and buy one of those pulse point bracelets and risk it? The sail isn't very long, and there aren't any storms due over the next day or two. You haven't been on a boat much in the past few years. Maybe you'll have grown out of being seasick?"

"But what if I am? I don't want to be puking into a bucket on a boat with strangers. It would be humiliating."

"You have to be willing to try things. You have to push yourself to do things out of your comfort zone. Yes, it's a risk to sail to the island, but as far as I know, you've only felt ill on boats three or four times, and that was when you were a lot younger. You've had plenty of occasions when you've been on a boat and felt fine, haven't you?"

Silence for a moment, then a reluctant, "Yes."

"So maybe the idea of being seasick isn't the thing that's holding you back from arriving on Kosmima on the yacht instead of the ferry. Maybe there's something more to it."

"It's one guy and three girls. And the girls are great sailors who flirt with Liam."

"But he asked you to marry him."

"He introduced me as his girlfriend, and he hasn't told them we're getting married. I don't know if he's having second thoughts."

Ella's heart squeezed at the pain in her daughter's voice. "Are you?"

"I don't know. We keep fighting. Liam wants to party and have fun. He's such an extrovert he makes friends everywhere we go and doesn't understand why I don't. We're in a group who all play games online in college. He asked me out before he ever saw me. We talk away all night as a gang when we're playing, and I guess I come over as more outgoing online. Being here has shown me a different side to Liam, and it's shown him a different side to me. I think we're both just realizing we don't know each other as well as we thought."

"You have time. Both of you have so much time on your side. Come to Kosmima, and we'll work out what to do next."

# Chapter Fourteen

Having a leisurely lunch on a Greek island with two gorgeous men was fun. They were such good friends that the atmosphere between the two was open and unguarded. The conversation flowed easily, and it was with a feeling of sadness Ella acknowledged that this would be one of the last times they'd be together on the island.

She had been lounging in her underwear, intent on seduction, when Aidan walked through the door at lunchtime.

To her mortification, Nick walked right in behind him. To her relief, he pretended he hadn't noticed her scantily-dressed mad dash for the stairs and greeted her warmly when she returned fully dressed.

The old Ella would never have been caught in such a compromising situation. Nick would assume she and Aidan had slept together. It shouldn't matter what Nick thought. But somehow, it did. Every summer, someone probably ended up in Aidan's bed. She didn't want Nick to think of her as merely another dig groupie, especially as Nick knew Liam and would meet Amber.

Nick greeted her with a smile and a fist bump. He explained that Aidan told him she would need to leave soon, so they'd decided to take the rest of the day off and give her a proper send-off.

To her delight, they all were in total agreement that surf and a delicious lunch would perfectly fit the bill. Now, after hours on the water they relaxed at a beachside restaurant. Calamari and fries, with tossed salads on the side, washed down with a couple of glasses of delicious red wine—could there be anything better?

The waitress brought out little plates of baklava.

*Yes, apparently*. Ella popped a small square into her mouth. "Oh, I love it." She couldn't help but smile.

A look passed between Nick and Aidan. One she couldn't interpret. The polite thing to do was to ignore it, but two glasses of wine and she was way past polite. "What?"

"What what?" Nick filled up her glass again.

"What was that look between you two? Is there something between my teeth?" She rubbed her tongue over them to check.

"I was telling Nick earlier that you were Trouble. I don't think he believed me."

"I believe him now." Nick clinked his glass against hers. "You're one hell of a surfer."

"I live in a beach house. Right on the beach. I love the water." A memory floated to the surface. She placed her hand over Aidan's forearm. "We always meant to go to Donegal to surf, do you remember?"

"Yes. Bundoran. I've been."

It was another of the things they planned to do together that he'd done and she hadn't. She'd taken a different path and missed so many things. Surfing in Cali and Greece must be way preferable to sinking into the ice-cold water of an Irish

October, squished into a wetsuit, but still. It was a memory she'd wanted to make and hadn't.

"I'll go one day. Bundoran."

"Or Kerry. Surf's great in Kerry, too. It's cold, but there's always whiskey in front of the fire afterward." Aidan shifted, bringing her attention to the fact that her hand was still resting on his warm arm. She took it away and reached for her wineglass.

"Would you like some coffee, Ella?" Nick asked, waving the waitress over.

"Not for me." She pushed back her chair. "I'll just use the facilities before we go."

After a quick consult with the waitress, she walked into the restaurant. On the way back out, she noticed a stack of linen for sale on a wooden table by the door. An older woman sitting close at the cash till encouraged her to investigate, so she unfolded the top one.

It was a small square tablecloth, beautifully embroidered with a pattern of waves, dolphins, and mermaids around the sides and the sun and clouds in the center.

"Go ahead! Look!" the woman urged so she unfolded the next and the next.

A magnificent bull with flowers woven through his horns. A Grecian woman holding him by a brightly colored halter. Another abstract design of flowers, with eagles, angels, and snakes.

"These are wonderful." Ella checked the card on top of the stack. A name and a telephone number, and a very reasonable price. She snapped a picture of the card with her phone. "Can I buy these two?" She selected her favorites and paid for them. "The woman who makes these, is she local?"

"My sister. She lives in the village."

"Thank you." Ella folded the cloths under her arm and walked out into the sunshine.

The restaurants, tavernas, and shops were closing for siesta. Nick was keen to get to Twin Pines to see Kitten so he drove to Nick's house to drop them off.

She stood in the driveway, watching the swirling dust as the Jeep left.

"Coming in?"

Aidan held the door open, and she squeezed past him into the cool sitting room.

"What did you buy?"

"Tablecloths. They're beautiful, look." She cleared the dining table and spread one of the cloths flat. "The embroidering is so fine." She traced a mermaid with her fingertip. "I just couldn't resist them."

"You want something to drink?" Aidan swung open the door of the fridge. "Water?"

"Sure." She felt pleasantly buzzed after all the wine, but hydration was probably a good idea. She folded up the cloth and opened the second one flat on the table. "Our customers would love these." She indulged a fantasy of a stack of embroidered cloths on the little table next to the door in *Precious Things* before harsh reality intruded. The ebullient mood that had been hers since the moment she ran into the waves that morning withered and died. "I don't know what I was thinking." She folded the cloths and stacked them on the edge of the table. "I must be mad. The shop is finished."

"Come sit down." Aidan took her elbow and steered her to the sofa.

He knew about the water damage, but they hadn't talked about her plans. The hard choices she had to make that would alter the course of her future forever.

And, much as it wasn't his problem, and burdening him with her concerns was more than a little impolite considering she would be leaving soon, she offloaded.

Every. Little. Detail.

He abandoned bringing her water and switched to wine. Set a fire in the hearth but didn't light it. Not watching her or making her feel self-conscious, but just giving her his attention naturally, in the way he'd always done.

Laying all the problems out like she laid out the embroidered tablecloths. Smoothing them down. Examining every single element.

"So, life sucks." She finished. "I don't want to sell my house, and the shop is in the building my grandmother left me. I feel like I've let her down if I sell, but I can't afford to buy Jason out."

Aidan leaned his back against the sofa. Twisted to look into her eyes. "You were really happy today—out there, surfing."

"I was."

"How long has it been since you surfed in California?"

"Years." She couldn't even remember how long it had been since she took to the water. Somehow she'd started thinking surfing was for people in their twenties. Jason considered surfers beneath him and had strongly discouraged her from taking out her board, and her mother's distaste for the sport had fortified his position.

"You stopped doing something that brings you total joy because of other people. Now you're feeling guilty about letting go of a building because your grandmother gave it to you."

His blue eyes blazed into hers. "Do something that makes you happy for once, Ell."

Spark joy. Keep only the things that spark joy. Ella had a flashback to the mound of clothes on her bed at the beach house. The Ricky Martin tee, and how that was a part of her past she wouldn't—couldn't—ever let go.

Ella leaned forward and kissed Aidan's mouth.

Do something that makes you happy.

Do someone who makes you happy.

Kissing Aidan lifted her mood and filled her with light. He was correct. She couldn't keep living her life for other people, conforming to their view of her. She'd made a life out of being predictably reliable, the one whose job it was to be an anchor in the storm of all the lives swirling around hers. She never drank too much. Never sang too loud. Never wore any swimsuit but a modest, black, age-appropriate one. She was a sober, sensible businesswoman and a devoted mother. But once upon a time, she was just Trouble. Wild, free, following her heart and living her best life.

Earlier today, she'd wondered where that woman went. But the answer sang loud and clear inside her as Aidan's arms wrapped around her, pulling her close as he deepened the kiss.

With a silent sigh, her defenses fell. This was perfection. Was enough. The lazy, languid way his fingers stroked her back, the feel of the springy hair at the nape of his neck beneath her fingertips, the press of their bodies against each other, all combined to focus her attention on what was happening between them.

She reveled in his touch. With every breath, she inhaled the scent of the sea on his skin. The world stilled to this place, to this moment.

He pulled away a fraction, breaking the connection. Aidan stroked his thumb along her jawline from chin to ear.

She opened her eyes to see him watching her with a faraway look in his gaze.

"We're here again." His voice was deep and soft, barely above a whisper.

They were right where they'd been that morning. Kissing Aidan was as natural as breathing.

* * *

There was something different about Ella. A determined gleam in her eyes that hadn't been there before.

"There are a million reasons why we shouldn't do this right now. I can't think any of them matter." Ella placed her hand flat on Aidan's chest. "With Amber and Liam arriving in the next couple of days, my time here has shrunk. I'll leave, and the next time we see each other might be at our children's wedding if they decide to continue on that path. This time is all we have. "

It didn't make any sense. If they wanted to be together, the question of distance should be no obstacle.

Her gaze was steady. "Let's go to bed. " He placed his hand over hers so she could feel his heartbeat, feel the effect her words had on him. "Are you sure?"

Whatever they decided to do now would be fun--he couldn't deny that. But there was so much history between them. They hadn't just been friends and involved in a casual relationship; she'd been his first real love, and he hers. Their romance had been a teenage thing; it couldn't possibly compare to the years he spent with Carol. But it had to count for something. And heaven help them both if they re-tangled their lives and lived to regret it.

"I've spent the last twenty years taking all the safe choices. This might be the last time I ever spend with you, and I don't want to wonder about what that might have been like—I want to live it."

He did, too. Ella's cornflower-blue eyes widened when he pulled her close. Then he lowered his head and did what both of them had been waiting for all day.

In his bedroom, she undressed slowly, placing her clothes on a chair and tucking her shoes under the bed before facing him, naked. She crossed her arms. Tilted her head to the side. A smile edged one side of her mouth upward. "Not the same body."

He stripped off his clothes, too. “Me neither.” He stroked a hand down her arm. “You’re beautiful.”

She stepped close. His arms went around her, and his eyes closed. He breathed in the scent of her hair. Feeling the shiver on her skin, her remembered curves fitting against his naked body as they had so many times in the past thrust him back through time.

Since Carol, the only women he’d been physically close to, had been casual hookups. Perfectly nice women, but ones who wanted the same thing that he did: a moment of intimacy without the strings. His body and brain had been involved, but not his feelings, not his heart.

Just holding Ella made emotion swell up within. She seemed to feel it, too. Her arms wove around his waist, and she rested her head against his chest, breathing unsteadily. Long before she raised her head to claim his mouth in a kiss, he was lost. They both were.

Her skin was soft and warm. Kissing her was like tumbling back through time. Once, she’d been everything. Now, the shadow of who she’d been to him faded, and the reality of her today was illuminated as if by a sunbeam. Now, being skin to skin with her was no longer a half-forgotten memory but a reality. Here and now.

They climbed into bed, she pushed him flat onto his back, and her long blonde hair brushed his chest as she ran her hands over him, then followed the trail she’d traced with her lips.

He moved. Her palm flattened on his chest. “Shh.”

She wanted him to stay put. Wanted to have control over this situation, to lead in this dance. He let her for as long as he could bear it, but eventually, he had to move. She grinned as he flipped their positions. A soft sigh escaped her parted lips when he kissed down her neck to her breast.

She arched her back. Aidan edged her legs apart and settled between them.

He wanted to take his time, to squeeze every last inch of pleasure out of their coming together. Because every moment was precious. Their passionate reunion had a time limit. Once Liam and Amber arrived, they'd have to pretend to be no more than concerned parents. Liam was curious enough about their relationship, and there was no way he would discuss Ella with his son.

But as he entered her, nothing but this experience, right now, mattered. Ella was everything. He felt like a teenager again, surfing a rush of hormones. They rolled, they tumbled, taking turns being on top. His world filled with labored breathing and frantic hands. Muttered words of excitement, of encouragement.

She gripped his shoulders so tight he was pretty sure her fingernails left half-moon dents in his skin.

"Aidan."

His eyes flicked open. Ella's eyes stared into the depths of his, with wonder and delight painted all over her face. His mouth curved into a smile. Then he kissed her again, and again, holding her tight as she tensed and then let the waves of her orgasm flood. He followed her seconds later, holding her close as though they were two survivors safe in the eye of a storm.

* * *

Sun, slanting through the window, woke Ella. She reached for the other side of the bed to find a warm indent where Aidan had lain. He was gone, but the sound of someone walking around downstairs and the aroma of coffee scented the air. She linked her fingers behind her head and stared at the ceiling.

Last night. She breathed in then let the breath out slowly. What had she done? Last night, going to bed with Aidan was inevitable. But this morning, doubts swooped and dived. For the first time in years, she wasn't in control. She had no plan and didn't know where, if anywhere, this was going. And she didn't care. She only knew one thing, that she had no regrets. Rather than wonder about the past, or stress about the future, she intended to live in the present.

For the next twenty-four hours anyway.

She filled a mug of coffee and joined Aidan on the terrace.

He walked over, tilted her face up with a finger under her chin, and kissed her. "Morning," he whispered against her lips.

Her heart hammered. She kissed him back. Somehow, she managed to put her coffee down on the table without spilling it.

"I wanted to take you to a secret beach the other day. While we were hiking." He retook his seat.

"Secret?"

"You can only see it from the sea. Nick and I found it one year when we were fishing. It's near that curve in the headland where we stood on the boulder. There's a hidden path that veers off through scrub."

"Sounds pretty private."

"It is." His lips curved into a slow smile she could not look away from. "You won't need a swimsuit." The intimate look in his eyes caught fire. "Unless you want to do something different...visiting the museum? Shopping?"

"Oh yes, I want to go shopping," she drawled, sarcastic. "You and I could be lounging around naked on a secret beach, but I think I want to go shopping." She walked over. "Or we could just stay here and close out the world."

They'd made love three times last night. She should be satisfied, but being with Aidan relit a fire within she hadn't even realized had gone out. In less than a week, she'd be out of here. Back to her old life, her old problems. The prospect of all the things she had to face was so unappealing she couldn't even bear to consider them.

"Bed?" Aidan asked.

"Hmm, we've done bed. How about the sofa?"

He followed her into the house and backed her up against the wall. "Next. The sofa comes next." He unbuttoned her shirt and pushed it from her shoulders. Unfastened his jeans. And cupped her breasts. His lips pressed against the column of her neck. "I can't get enough of you."

"Me neither. Keep trying."

Later, they found the beach. They swam in the clear turquoise water for a while, then retreated to the towel Aidan had placed on the firm sand above the waterline. He sat staring out to sea, and she sat between his legs, her back to his front. In the circle of his arms, the overwhelming feeling was of togetherness. Intimacy.

With the heat of his body at her back, she told him everything that had happened since her marriage broke down. Like writing thoughts in a diary or talking to a non-judgmental best friend; she left nothing out. The freedom of voicing past hurts and confessing present cares for an unknown future was freeing.

He listened silently. And when she finally ran out of words, she leaned back against his body and closed her eyes.

"Come on. It's time to go."

She twisted to look at him. "So soon?"

"We've been here for hours. I want to buy some supplies before siesta."

"Okay." She pulled on her tee-shirt and wrapped a skirt around her waist.

When they had packed up their things, he took her hand. "Your life is complicated. Mine is, too." He glanced at the ground as they walked up the narrow path. "I lecture half the year and spend the rest traveling. Three months in the summer on digs—the rest of the time setting up new projects. I don't have much time for relationships."

"I understand that. "

He pulled her close and kissed her. "I wish we had longer."

# Chapter Fifteen

The moment they walked into Aidan's house, alerts on both of their phones pinged.

"What the hell?" Aidan glanced at the screen. "Liam." He strode across the room, phone glued to his ear.

Ella's screen was filled with missed calls and texts from Amber. She scanned them quickly.

*Where are you?*

*Call me back.*

*Call Amber straight away, then call me*—from Louise.

Her heart raced, and her mouth was dry as she placed the call.

"Mom. Thank god, where were you?"

Amber didn't sound injured or desperate, so some of Ella's tension dissipated. "I was at the beach. There's very little signal anywhere on the island, remember?"

"I know, I know. It's just...I've been calling you for hours. There's been a change of plans. I'm not coming to Kosmima."

"Are you okay? Has there been an accident? Is Liam with you?" Every possible possibility flashed through Ella's mind.

Questions crowded her head, but she forced herself to stop talking and just listen.

"I'm not getting married. He's just—"Amber's voice broke, and Ella cast a glance to the other side of the room where Aidan was pacing while speaking to Liam.

"He's what? What did Liam do? Did he hurt—"

"No, Mum. Of course, he didn't." She was silent for a moment, forming sentences in her mind before speaking. As she always did. "We want different things. We didn't think getting married through properly. He wants to take up an internship in Berlin and didn't see how that would affect me. Where am I supposed to be in all his plans? He lives with his dad in Dublin. We'd planned on moving out, but rents are so high, and I'd have to work, and—" She broke off with a frustrated sigh. "I'm not ready for this."

"Okay, so come meet me in Kosmima, and we'll travel home together."

"I can't. I can't bear to meet Liam's father now. And I don't want to see Liam. At least not for a while. He'll be in Kosmima tomorrow, and I'm in Thessaloniki airport, waiting to board a flight to Dublin in an hour."

"Amber—"

"I want to go home, Mom. I just want to go home. I've booked a flight from Dublin to Monterey four hours after landing in Dublin, so I won't even be leaving the airport. I called Louise and asked her to pick me up."

"I can't make that flight." Maybe there was a direct flight from Athens. "But I'll follow you as quickly as I can. How are you for funds? Do you need me to transfer some money?"

"No, I'm okay. You sent me the fare, remember, and I can dip into the emergency fund if I need to. They're calling me to the gate now. I better go."

"Call me when you get to Dublin. I'll be here."

Aidan opened the patio door and strode backward and

forward in the warm evening air, talking animatedly on his phone.

Ella called Louise.

"You spoke to Amber?" Louise didn't bother with small talk.

"I'm just off the phone now." She sat on the sofa and kicked off her shoes. "I wasn't expecting that."

"Me either."

"I feel so bad she couldn't contact me. I was at the beach."

"There's no signal, she knows that, and in case she'd forgotten, I reminded her when we spoke. So don't feel guilty. There's nothing you could have done differently. When she couldn't reach you, she waited half an hour and called me." She yawned. "At two-thirty in the morning."

"I'm sorry."

"It's okay. What are godmothers for? She organized flights, and I will pick her up from the airport. I'll take her to my house and keep an eye on her until you get home."

"Jason can—"

"Amber told me she's embarrassed. She doesn't want to see her father right now."

"Okay, fair enough. I don't know when I'll get home; I'll have to travel to a bigger island to find an airport. I'll text you my flight details when I have them."

"No panic. I'll take good care of her. Travel safe."

Ella dropped her phone onto the sofa and rubbed at her closed eyes.

"Do you want wine? Because I am having wine." Aidan slid the door shut behind him.

She followed him into the kitchen where they filled two large glasses.

"Holy hell. Liam was in a state. He said Amber got a taxi to the airport. Is she okay?"

"She's fine. She's getting on a plane back to Dublin and

then straight on to Monterey. I have to get home. Can I use your laptop to look at flights?'

"There's time for that. Have a drink." He took his glass to the sitting area and sprawled onto the sofa. "I've heard Liam's story. What did Amber say happened?"

"She said he wants to do an internship in Berlin. That he hadn't considered her in his plans."

"She doesn't expect him to not go, does she? Liam applied for the internship, but didn't think he'd get it. It's perfect for him—he can't throw it away just because his girlfriend disapproves."

Ella drank wine. Tried to get her temper under control. "She was more than his girlfriend. They planned to get married. And Liam didn't seem to give much of a damn about Amber throwing her studies away for him. They'd planned to get a flat, and from what I gather, she was the only one who would be bringing in an income."

Aidan's jaw was set in a firm line. He was clenching his teeth. "If she wanted to do that, she was crazy." He leaned back and crossed his arms. "You would be crazy to let her quit college to live with Liam under those circumstances."

"Exactly." She moved to the sofa. "That's why I'm here. To make her see sense. She's okay, she's upset, but she's holding it together. She said Liam is coming straight here?"

"He's sailing with some new friends."

"Maybe he and Amber can work it out."

"I don't know. Liam told a different story." He rubbed his hand through his hair. "I think there was more to their breakup than his internship offer. They'd been inter-railing through the Greek islands, living in hostels and hanging out with other student travelers. Liam's gregarious. He thrives on the social scene. He told me he drank too much on Rhodes, and she had to ask someone they met at a bar to help get him back to the hostel." He grimaced. "I'm not happy about it, but he's young. It's the first time he's been away on holiday before, and I guess he hasn't learned to hold his drink."

"Amber's shy. She'd find that difficult."

Aidan nodded. "Liam said she was upset the following day. They had a fight and seemed to get over it, but things went south again when he wanted to go to Thessaloniki. The plan had initially been to visit Santorini and continue on to us, but Liam wanted to change things around.

"Liam's obsessed with architecture. They detoured to Thessaloniki, but when they got there, she wanted to find a laundry, and he had a list of buildings he wanted to see. He couldn't understand why she'd voluntarily lock herself away in a launderette washing her clothes rather than visit World Heritage sites."

"And Amber wouldn't understand how he could pass up the chance of getting clean clothes." It was apparent that the teens were very different people.

Aidan poured them another glass of wine. "The email about the internship was the last straw. They argued, then she caught a cab to the airport."

* * *

They stood on the dock, Ella's suitcases at their feet. A snaking queue of people ambled to the passenger ferry, but she made no move to join it. There was still too much unsaid. Too much important stuff to say that neither of them seemed able to voice.

"I've got your number. I'll call when I get home." She fiddled with the strap of her handbag. "I don't know what time that'll be. Of course, if it's late, I won't call, and if it's during the day, you'll be up at the site, so I won't be able to reach you—" There was desperation in her eyes. Her shoulders slumped. "I don't know what to say."

She'd spent the previous evening on his laptop, checking for flights. It wasn't easy finding one at such short notice, especially considering she needed to factor travel from Kosmima into her plans.

But finally, after the bottle of wine was drunk and her credit card had received a thorough pounding, Ella closed the laptop and declared the job done.

Neither of them spoke about the future. He didn't know what future they could have. They lived in different countries, and even though this time together had been fun, how well did they really know each other two decades later?

Instead, they made love late into the night, letting their bodies say what their mouths wouldn't.

"Do you have to rush off? Why not wait until tomorrow? Your friend is picking Amber up at the airport."

She was walking out of his life again, but this time he was standing here watching her go. Without being able to stop her.

"In half an hour, my ship will have sailed. And soon after, the yacht bringing Liam will arrive." She touched the side of his face. "I have to get home. It's not just Amber. There's a whole world of pain I've been avoiding. I need to work out what I'm doing with my life."

He pulled her close. "I'll miss you." He pressed his mouth to hers, putting all the things he couldn't say into his kiss. That despite his best intentions, he'd lost perspective and was feeling a familiar ache in his chest at the knowledge that what was between them was over—again.

Most of the passengers had already boarded. Only a few stragglers remained, saying goodbye to their loved ones. With a tight smile, Ella lifted her suitcases. "I won't be up on deck. Once I've boarded, I'll find somewhere to sit." She walked away, climbed up the gangplank, and didn't look back.

Aidan walked to a nearby café and ordered coffee. He

watched from a table as the stately white ship set out into the blue.

* * *

Ella hadn't pulled the drapes when she arrived back last night, so the sun streaming in through the window woke her. It had only been weeks since she left. But it felt so much longer.

She looked around, seeing the room with different eyes. Everything was inoffensively white. White walls. White rug. No pictures on the wall and white bedding. As though she'd bleached out any sign of individuality. A year ago, she'd packed up all her belongings in cardboard boxes when she left the house she shared with Jason. She'd unpacked kitchen essentials, but so much of the remainder held unhappy memories of a life that wasn't hers anymore. She'd left the boxes unopened —unable to move forward, but unable to discard them either. She pretended she was over her marriage breakup. That she was bravely moving on with her life. But the truth was, she was in limbo.

There were a lot of things in those boxes that meant something. That felt like her, not just like bad memories.

She picked up her phone and checked the time. Still early. She'd called Louise before the plane took off and passed on her travel details. Louise would drop Amber home when she woke up, and there was no way Ella could get back to sleep now.

She wandered into the kitchen and made some coffee. Then carried it into the spare room and opened the first box.

She stopped when Amber and Louise walked in three hours later.

"How are you doing, honey?" She crossed the room and enveloped her daughter in a hug. Then she turned to Louise. "Want some coffee? I'll put the machine on."

Louise shook her head. "No, I won't stay. I'll catch up

with you later." She handed over a white cake box. "Sustenance. Until you get to the store." She darted a telling look at the back of Amber's head. "See you, Amber."

"Thanks for everything." Amber hugged Louise, then walked into the kitchen and began opening and closing cupboards.

"She's not great," Louise muttered under her breath. "I can't get her to talk, and she's been very withdrawn."

Amber had always needed to work through her problems on her own before sharing her opinions about things, so Ella wasn't surprised at Louise's words. "Okay." She walked her friend to the door and hugged her again. "Thanks."

When she returned to the sitting room, Amber sat nursing a cup of herbal tea.

"Let's sit outside." Ella slid the door open and stepped out into the sunlight. Fresh air would do them both good.

They sat for a while looking out at the sparkling water.

Ella wiggled her toes in the warm sand. "I think buying this place was the best decision I made for a long time."

Amber looked up, surprised.

"I love the water. Before I left to go to college, I surfed every day. I was organizing the spare room and I found my old surfboard." She turned and pointed to the surfboard she'd leaned up against the back wall of the beach house. "I think I'll test it out after breakfast."

A tiny frown line creased above Amber's eyes. "Are you feeling okay, Mom? Do you think you still remember how?"

"I know I do. I spent some great days surfing on Kosmima."

"With Liam's father?"

She nodded. "Yes, with Aidan. And with his friend Nick. I remembered how much I loved it and how much I missed it."

"You're different." Amber tilted her head to the side and examined her mother closely. "Less...stiff, somehow."

"I feel different. Or at least different from the way that I've felt for the past few years. I feel more like I used to be." There were so many things she hadn't talked to Amber about. She'd been trying so hard to not involve her in her and Jason's messy marriage breakdown that she put up a front that everything was all right. As a result, they somehow stopped communicating honestly.

She shook out her hands. "I'm sorry your engagement is off. I know it must hurt."

Amber leaned forward, so her long blonde hair swung in front of her face, partially hiding it from view. "I know I made some bad choices. I should have known better."

"Hey." Ella reached out and touched Amber's arm. Amber looked up. "I haven't been honest with you. I've let you believe I think things through before I make decisions and that I'm always happy about how things work out. I've been overprotective and tried to shield you from any messy feelings, but the truth is, everyone makes bad choices sometimes. Both me and your father made some terrible ones. And that's okay. That's life. It doesn't mean we shouldn't talk about them."

"I've wanted to talk about Dad and Betsy. Louise says I should speak to you about them; she says you would want me to."

"Yes, sure." This was new. Amber hadn't talked much about her father's new relationship.

"They're getting married, and he told me not to tell you because he didn't want you to be upset." She crossed her arms. "Which is really patronizing bullshit. His ego is out of control."

"I suspected he was getting married again." She made a definite attempt not to minimize her feelings. "And yes, it hurts. Because it doesn't seem that long since we divorced, and we were together for a long time. But he's been with Betsy since we split, and I'm not surprised that they've decided to move on to the next stage." She smiled. "I'm not about to break into pieces. I'll survive. I have no desire to ever be with your father again. I'd like for us to be friends because it makes it easier to co-parent but beyond that...."

Amber swallowed. "He was with Betsy before." She cast Ella a nervous glance. "Wasn't he?"

Something about the way she said the words hinted that Amber hadn't just suspected; she knew. "Yes, they started before we officially split." There was no need to go into the depths of Jason's infidelity. Amber was still his daughter.

"I saw Betsy having coffee with Dad in town." Amber spoke low and haltingly. "A couple of months before you both told me you were getting a divorce. I should have told you. I'm sorry."

She'd only been a teenager. Keeping her father's secret had eaten her up from the inside.

"You didn't need to tell me. And it's okay that you didn't. There's a lot I didn't tell you, too."

Amber leaned back and swung her hair away from her face. She looked freer than she had for ages. Her whole demeanor had changed. "Yeah, I had to hear about your flashing from my boyfriend."

"If you want to hear my side of that story, we'll need coffee. And cake."

# Chapter Sixteen

FOUR WEEKS LATER

The door to *Precious Things* was open wide, and the shop was packed to capacity. Ella and Louise mingled with their customers, passing out new business cards and talking.

A banner proclaiming 'Closing Down' hung above the door, and the windows and tabletops were decorated with fliers.

Amber and a couple of her friends circulated in the crowd, explaining what was next for the shop.

"Take a picture of this square." Amber pointed at the Q code at the corner of the flier. "And our new website comes up." She demonstrated with the woman's phone. "And take a flier, too." She pointed at a pile stacked on the table. "There's a special discount here for our loyal customers who buy from the website. It's only available to the people who are here today."

The woman picked a couple of fliers off the table and handed one to her friend. "We've been coming here for years. Your mother and Louise have such exquisite taste." She looked around. "I love these new tablecloths from Greece. Are they part of the sale stock, too?"

"Yes. Everything is reduced today. But remember, after today, you'll have to order from the website."

Pride swelled in Ella's chest as she watched her daughter engage with another shopper. She'd always been shy and reticent to come forward, but she was right in her element here today.

"It's going well." Louise appeared at her elbow. "Maybe some of the people are just window shopping—"

"But it's all good." She gestured to the door where a couple of local teenagers they hired for the day were waving new cars in through the entrance and helping them park. "People filling the space builds buzz. And buzz encourages shopping." She looked over to the register. "Alison is overwhelmed. I better go and help."

Their friend had closed *Carthago* early to help out. She'd bought their last two small decorative tables for her gallery at half-price. The only piece of furniture unsold was the giant dresser stacked with china against the back wall.

"Are there any more of these teacups?" Alison held one up from behind the register. "This lady would like some more."

"How many?"

"Well, they're half price, so...do you have another six?"

"Let me just get them. Could you stand to one side for a moment and let Alison serve another customer? I promise I won't be long."

The woman obediently moved. Ella wove through the crowd to the dresser and picked up the last seven cups and matching saucers, then made her way back to the counter.

"There's only one more. I'll throw it in for free." The woman smiled. "Thank you so much!" She picked up a flier from the cash desk.

Ella noticed a familiar face entering the building and dashed over to greet her realtor.

"Coming to pick up a bargain?" She smiled.

Sandy had been as good as her word and found the perfect buyer for their premises. The new owner wanted to transform the shop into a restaurant and had been willing to pay well for the privilege.

"Well, there are a few things I've always liked." Sandy looked around the room. "Is the drinks trolley still here? I've had my eye on it since the first day I came in here."

"You're in luck." Ella marched to the golden trolley and started taking glasses off it. She handed a gold soda siphon to Sandy. "You must take this, too. They're made for each other." She was about to move the trolley across the room when a tall young man stepped in. "Let me do that, Mrs. Blackstone."

"Thanks, Kyle. And please stop calling me Mrs. Blackstone. My name's Ella."

"Ella." Kyle had known her since he was a twelve-year-old kid in Amber's class. Once they'd started working on their plan to give the business a new lease of life online, he'd been instrumental. He was studying computer science and enthusiastically agreed to build the website with Amber's help.

"So you won't be selling furniture or rugs any longer?" Sandy asked.

"I anticipate we'll still have some stock to take to our lock-up, but once that's sold, no. We're shifting the focus to smaller items we can ship easily and cheaply. They formed the bulk of our sales anyway. *Precious Things* was always supposed to be about beautiful objects produced by artisans, and that's our focus going forward."

"I love those new things you brought back from Greece."

"There will be some more items going up on the website soon—I'm awaiting the next shipment from the co-operative on Kosmima."

"Are we still okay for Wednesday?"

Vacant possession of the store was to happen in less than a week. Ella was ready to let her grandmother's gift go. It had been given to her so she would have options. So she would be able to follow her dreams. Over the years, her plans had changed. *Precious Things* could be administrated online, and she, Louise, or any assistant they employed could deal with worldwide shipping. She didn't need to be tied to one place any longer.

Traveling to Kosmima in search of her daughter had reignited a passion for visiting other places—to spread her wings and soar. She'd even taken the first steps by booking flights for herself and Louise. They'd start in Athens, then continue to Kosmima and build solid supplier relationships with the artisans in the co-operative.

"Yes. I'll meet you at nine."

* * *

Someone was shouting.

Aidan jerked awake. He lay for a moment, settling into his surroundings. Glanced at the alarm clock on the bedside table. Listened.

A shout rang out again. Now that Aidan was fully awake, he recognized the raised voice as Liam's coming from the room next door. His son was talking loudly and laughing. He must be playing a game online with his headphones on.

Aidan groaned and turned on his side. Four in the morning. Too soon to get up and go to work; too late to expect to get any worthwhile sleep.

"Oh, they got you! They got you!" Liam's voice was filled with glee.

Aidan kicked off the sheet and strode into the corridor. "Keep it down."

Liam continued laughing like a maniac. His noise-canceling headset was doing exactly as advertised.

Aidan opened the door.

Liam jumped. "Jesus, Dad!" His eyes widened and he pulled off his headset. "What are you doing just walking in here? I thought you were asleep."

"I was. Your shouting woke me up." He rubbed his eyes. "I've got to get up in a few hours and go to work. Just keep it down, would you?"

Liam's head jerked back and forward rapidly. "Yes, I'm sorry."

"Four in the morning, Liam."

"Sorry."

Aidan walked out and closed the door behind him. There was no point in going back into bed now; he wouldn't sleep. So instead, he headed down the corridor to the kitchen. There was a machine-gun clatter of rain on the roof. It was still dark, but he could see water spilling from the gutters and flooding the porch outside. There would be no working at the dig today if this kept up. The trenches would be waterlogged. It was impossible to work in flooded trenches. It was doubtful if anyone would turn up even if the weather improved.

Liam walked in twenty minutes later and made himself a sandwich. "I thought you would go back to bed."

"Couldn't sleep. What game were you playing?"

"The Treasure Hunter game. The one where you and your friends are running through the jungle being chased by cannibals. It's intense. I'm sorry I woke you."

"It's okay. Were you playing with friends from college?"

Liam poured a glass of orange juice and joined Aidan at the table. "Yes, four of us. From all over the world. Amber was there, too."

"Amber?" Liam hadn't mentioned his ex-fiancée for a couple of weeks, and Aidan hadn't probed. His son had been upset and depressed that his relationship ended, so Aidan tried his best to keep Liam busy and distracted with work at the site. "I didn't know you'd been in touch."

"This was the first time since—since we split." Liam swallowed his orange juice in one gulp. "She's part of the team in the game. It wouldn't be right to exclude her, or to not turn up. We need to get past the breakup."

"That sounds sensible."

"She told me she's coming back next year and keeping on with her studies. It was sort of awkward talking to her, but it was okay. And it will get better. We were friends before we were a couple. I'd like to get back to that."

"She's doing okay, then?" He itched to ask for more details of what was going on over there in Monterey. To ask if her mother ever talked about him. To find out what had happened in her life since she left.

He picked up his phone. Absentmindedly checked his photo reel, as had become a habit over the past month.

"I think so." Liam leaned close. "What's that?"

"Oh, nothing." Aidan turned his phone facedown on the table. "Just, uh, pictures."

"Is that her? Can I see?" Without waiting for Aidan's reply, Liam reached for the phone. He flicked through the pictures, paying rapt attention. One of Aidan and Ella at the port standing next to the ferry, faces close together and smiling. Ella had waved over a stranger and asked her to take the picture, then forwarded it to his phone so they'd both have a copy. One he took of her running onto the beach carrying the surfboard, her blonde hair salt-spray damp and curling. One of them on the day of the hike, sitting in the restaurant with the group. And finally, a selfie he'd taken. Staring straight into the camera. While she sat as close as a person could before actually sitting on someone. Her profile was to the camera, and she was looking at his face with an expression he couldn't define.

Was it caring? Wanting? They weren't touching, but the intimacy between them was unmistakable. And Liam was bearing witness.

Shame flooded Aidan in a wave. He wanted to reach for the phone. To hide the evidence of his attraction to a woman who wasn't Liam's mother from his son's eyes. Liam knew he'd dated since Carol's death, but this was something different. There was deep and genuine emotion woven into his relationship with Ella. He hadn't thought anyone apart from them would be aware of it, but the evidence was plain in all of these pictures. The way they looked together—complicit—was obvious.

Liam put the phone down. "You look happy."

"I guess."

Liam picked up the phone once more and flicked to the photo of Ella and Aidan in the restaurant. He zoomed in on her face. "Ella was in Trinity at the same time as you, so she was there at the same time as Mum, right?"

Aidan grunted.

"I've seen her." Liam lit up like a Christmas tree. "I'm sure I've seen her before, in Mum's photos."

The skepticism must have been plain on Aidan's face because Liam talked faster. "Before I started college, I went into the case in the back of your wardrobe with all your photos. I wanted..." He chewed his lip, embarrassed. "I wanted to see where Mum had gone when she was there. I thought I'd be walking in her footsteps, and I wanted to be able to picture her doing the same things."

There was a tight tug in Aidan's chest that his son had wanted to see those pictures and hadn't shared the experience.

Liam darted him a glance. "I didn't want to upset you."

Aidan understood. "It's okay."

"I took photos of some of them on my phone. I'll show you." He darted into the bedroom and came back seconds later. "Here." He scooted his chair close and showed the screen. He flicked through pictures of Carol as she had been before Aidan first saw her. With her parents in the college quad. Away from home for the first time in her college accommodation. Then less posed, at a bar they frequented around the corner from the college, Carol laughing in the middle of a group of people. Clutching a pint of stout.

He smiled at that one. He didn't recognize anyone else in the picture; it must have been the year before they met because Carol hadn't cut her hair yet.

"Keep flicking," Liam said. "There's a couple more."

He did as asked and then stopped.

"There. That one." Liam's excitement was off the charts. "Isn't that her?" The group photo was posed. Someone in the front row was holding a board that said 'Cinema Soc.' Carol was dead center in the front, but Liam was right. At the back, head tilted to one side was someone he'd never been able to forget. Trouble.

* * *

Ella stacked the remaining boxes into the back of her car. The job of sorting and clearing the cartons from the spare room had been a long time coming, but with persistent effort and an organized daughter holding her accountable, she finally managed it.

Every time she left the house, she filled the car with boxes and dropped them off at Goodwill. This was the last of them. She'd rethought the idea of having a spare room, too. Anyone she wanted to spend time with lived nearby. Back when she and Jason lived in the house on the hill, they had space to spare. But the beach house was different. Every inch was valuable.

So instead, its future role would be that of a home office. A pretty mahogany desk from the sale at *Precious Things* now graced one wall. And on the other was a new sofa bed so the room could do double duty as a bedroom if need be.

She shoved the boxes back a little and closed the trunk.

Amber walked out of the house. "Can you give me a lift to Kyle's? We want to take pictures of the new stock to update the website."

They drove in companionable silence. Ella listened to music while Amber flicked through things on her phone.

"I spoke to Liam last night."

Ella concentrated on the road ahead. "I didn't think you were in contact."

"We've spoken a couple of times. A group of us play the game together."

"Ah. And how is it? Okay?" The easiest way to stop Amber from talking was to ask too many questions, so Ella kept them to a minimum.

"Yes, it's okay. I still feel sad about how things went down, but I'm looking forward to going back to college. Working on the website has been good experience. I'm excited about next semester."

The road was too twisty to risk a glance, but Ella patted Amber's hand as it was within reach. "I'm so glad."

"Yeah, me, too." Amber hesitated. "He talked about his father."

"Aidan?" That was a surprise. She'd called him a few times, but he was terse and reticent to talk on the phone. She got the distinct impression that he felt whatever was between them was best left to die. She had no intention of leaving it there, though. She wanted to see him face to face to make that judgment.

"You really like him, don't you?"

The new policy of total honesty had to be adhered to. "Yes. I really do." She pulled in a deep breath. "Louise and I are going to Kosmima in a few weeks. I need to introduce her to our suppliers and hopefully expand our product line." She turned right and pulled up outside Kyle's apartment.

"This isn't anything to do with getting Dad's wedding invitation in the post this morning, is it?"

Two ivory cards had arrived that morning. One to Amber, which was expected—she'd already agreed to be a bridesmaid. But the invitation to Ella was unexpected. She'd been getting on much better with Jason since the matter of the shop had been settled, but there was no way in hell she'd go to that wedding.

"No. It's business. But I will use the opportunity to see Aidan. I guess I've been thinking that life is too short to wonder or regret not taking a chance. I need to see if there's any future for the two of us. I've been gathering the courage to call and tell him I'm coming back, but I can't read him. He's not giving me much over the phone."

"Liam says he's depressed. He found him looking through photos of you on his phone, and he thinks he definitely misses you. Nick wants Liam to persuade Aidan to go out, but he's staying close to home. Just traveling to the site and back every evening."

Could he be missing her just as she had been missing him? Ella had been waking early and heading out into the sea with the surfboard before breakfast every morning. She imagined him with her, in the water and out of it. When she sat on a towel on the beach, hugging her knees and gazing out over the white-capped waves, she imagined the heat of his body at her back. His arms around her.

She tempered the memories and the ache of missing him with the practical knowledge that they lived in different countries. That there was no way a relationship could survive those constraints.

"Last week, we talked about what I want to do in the future, Mom. And you told me to follow my dreams, that I can do anything. You believe that one hundred percent, I know you do."

"I do."

"So why don't you believe that for yourself? You're putting up barricades as if your future isn't as important as mine, and it is. I've never even met Aidan. Liam says he's looked at pictures of the two of you. Can I see?"

Ella felt heat flush her face but reached for her phone anyway. Aidan wasn't the only one who'd been looking at the photos and remembering.

She showed the pictures to Ella. One that she'd retrieved from twenty years ago and put onto her phone since she returned from Kosmima.

"Look at the two of you—you were kids!"

Ella grinned.

"You look so at ease with each other."

The apartment door opened and Kyle stepped out. Amber handed back the phone and opened the car door. "You should call him."

# Chapter Seventeen

Aidan and Nick lay on sun loungers shaded by a navy-blue sail on the white terrace of their rental villa in Santorini. Nick cracked open a beer.

"What time is Ophelia picking us up?"

"Four. She has organized a private tour of the settlement, and then we're meeting the rest of the team."

Aidan had visited the prehistoric settlement here many times, but it never got old. There was so much to see at Akrotiri and always too little time. Ophelia was part of the permanent staff and involved in the new project she wanted them to sign up for the following year. When they'd visited Kosmima, she'd extended an invitation, and Nick enthusiastically took her up on it.

"I hope my son doesn't trash the place while I'm away."

Nick slanted him a look. "I thought your mood would improve once I got you off the island, but the opposite seems to be true. Why are you in such a shit mood, man? Are you still missing Ella?"

"No." Aidan swallowed a mouthful of beer. "That's over."

"Huh. Ella might not be here, but that doesn't mean it's over."

Aidan stood and walked to the edge of the terrace. He rested his arms on the white walls and stared out to the caldera. "It's over. Believe me. She called me two nights ago, telling me she planned to come back in a couple of weeks for a visit. To talk about our future."

He drained the beer and put it down on the ground.

"I told her we didn't have a future. It had been fun, but that's all. I don't have anything else to give." He rubbed the back of his head. "We'll be here for a couple of days. I should unpack."

"What the hell are you talking about, man? You like her. You more than like her; you're totally hung up on her. Everyone's noticed—"

"I was married." There was a sour taste in Aidan's mouth. "I was married to Carol for decades. I thought I knew everything about her, but now I find myself questioning if she could have been given a letter by Ella years ago and destroyed it. I have doubts about my life with Carol. She called Ella 'the one that got away' and joked that she caught me on the rebound. It was just a joke. She never knew Ella—except by reputation. At least, that's what I always thought."

Nick frowned. "How did that change? I don't get it."

"Ella told me she passed a note to someone who was in one of the societies she was in and asked them to give it to me. Liam found a photo of the cinema society with both Carol and Ella in it." He stalked around the terrace.

"So you ask Ella if she—"

"No." Aidan crossed his arms. "I ask Ella nothing. I don't want to think that Carol had anything to do with Ella and me not finding each other again. I feel bad enough." It was evident from Nick's expression that he still didn't understand Aidan's reasoning. "I love her. And being with her again made me realize how I've always loved her. I was happy with Carol, but the feelings I have for Ella are different. Stronger." He lowered his head and stared at the cobalt-blue tiles. "Carol deserved more." He looked at his friend's face again.

"I'm going for a shower."

* * *

Nick cast an assessing eye over Ophelia's Fiat 500.

Ophelia looked at them, then at the car, and shrugged, with a pink blush painting her cheeks. "I was to bring my partner's car, it's bigger. But Spiros got up early this morning and took his car as usual." She skimmed them head to toe again. "I can call for someone to come from the settlement, or—it isn't far, so perhaps I can bring one of you at a time." She pulled down the hem of her white shirt.

"We can both fit." Nick opened the door. There is space behind the driver's seat, and Aidan can put his legs to the side. If we push the front passenger seat all the way back, I can squeeze in."

"It's ten minute's drive. Max."

Aidan stood back and watched Nick work the angles. The front seat situation worked, but there was no way Nick could fit in the backseat.

"How about I drive, and you sit behind me?"

Ophelia gratefully agreed. "Have you both visited Akrotiri before?"

"Of course." Nick peered into the back of the tiny car and started an animated conversation about the world-famous excavated town while Aidan drove, hunched over the steering wheel.

Ophelia was right, their destination was only minutes away, but relief flooded Aidan as he prised himself from the car, like a snail from a shell.

"I'll ask one of the other archaeologists to drive you back later." Ophelia took the keys he offered. "As you've already been here, I won't give you the standard tour. You can just ask me any questions. I love the frescos, so we'll start there. The newest areas of excavation are not available for the general public to view, but we are meeting the rest of the team there, and they will walk you through our discoveries."

The excavated city spanned over fifty acres. Much of it was covered by a roof and thus protected from the elements and available to view no matter the weather. They wandered from area to area marveling at the extraordinary ancient city. Ophelia walked them into the room containing the Spring Fresco and excused herself to consult a passing guide.

"The team asked me to work with them next spring," Nick said, quietly. "Part of the purpose of this trip was to give them my answer."

Nick spent most of the year in Athens, only spending his summers on Kosmima. Relocating permanently was a significant departure.

"What about our project? Are you out of that?"

"I'll continue working the summers in Kosmima. I can split the time between here and there."

"Why didn't you tell me?" Even as he said the words, Aidan could guess the answer. He'd been distracted while Ella was on the island and reclusive since she left. Nick had tried to drag him out for a meal or a drink for weeks, but he stubbornly refused.

He forced a weak smile. "No need to answer that. I know I haven't been easy to talk to."

"I'm moving in with Kitten." Nick shoved his hands in his pockets. "I didn't want to rub your face in our happiness, but I didn't want to spend the next few months waiting for the summer to come around again. Not when we can be together.

It won't be easy living on different islands for part of the year, but it will be worth it."

Aidan thumped his friend on the back. "I'm happy for you."

Ophelia walked in their direction.

Nick stared into Aidan's eyes. "You could be happy too, mate. Call Ella back."

* * *

"Do you want to call him again?"

Louise picked up one of the small bowls of olives on the table next to their cocktails and started snacking.

They spent three days in Athens, breathing in the ambiance and acclimatizing. Ella wanted to go and see the Meteora rock formations at Kalambaka and visit the monasteries. But Louise could take them or leave them, so she decided to schedule that for another trip. Hopefully, with someone equally fascinated by archeology.

They managed a trip to the Acropolis. A thorough check out of all the shops. And indulged in all the nightlife Athens had to offer. Tonight was the last night in their four-star hotel, and tomorrow early, they would be catching the ferry to Kosmima.

"I tried about an hour ago. No luck."

It was impossible to know if Aidan was ignoring her or just not receiving her calls. Since he'd been adamant that things were over between them, she suspected the former.

"I won't call him again. We'll visit the dig site and take it from there. He'll either want to talk or tell me to get lost. I'm glad you're with me. I won't feel quite as pathetic as I would if I were on my own."

Louise poured some more margarita from the cocktail

shaker. "No one could think you were remotely pathetic. You're a businesswoman meeting your suppliers on a Greek island and forging more intimate working relationships. You're fucking fabulous." She sipped her drink. "As we have to catch that ferry tomorrow at eight, let's be lazy and just eat in the hotel tonight."

When she walked off the ferry the following morning, Ella looked at the island anew. On her previous visit, she'd barely noticed her surroundings. Her primary focus had been to try to find somewhere to stay and then to track down Amber. She'd been focused and determined. But now, things were different.

Now, she could slow down and smell the roses.

She set her bags on the ground. Closed her eyes and tilted her head up to the sun.

"Where are the cabs?" Louise frowned. "How will we get to the hotel?"

Ella picked up her things. "We walk."

She'd suggested that her friend bring comfortable footwear before they left, but Louise had looked at her, uncomprehending for a minute before asking if she meant flats. On hearing that's exactly what Ella meant, Louise laughed and shook her head.

Now, she dragged her suitcase on the rough cobbles and tried to keep her ankles steady on the dimpled surface.

Ella caught a glimpse of the fabric awnings of the weekend market through a gap in the buildings. "We can walk down to the market and pick up some espadrilles once we've checked in."

Louise pulled a face.

"They did have gorgeous leather gladiator sandals too—with those straps that go right up to your knee."

"Gold or silver ones?" Louise looked slightly more interested, but only slightly. She picked her way over the cobbles.

"Because I could manage those." She frowned. "How much further is this hotel?"

"Five or ten minutes." Ella spotted a bench a little distance away, in front of the cake shop. "Come over here." She settled her friend on the seat and popped into the shop. A few minutes later, she deposited a small white bag in her friend's hands. "Here. Some baklava. Stay put and don't get into any trouble. I'll run down and buy you a pair of those sandals."

"Gold ones if they have them." Louise opened the bag.

"Ella, you're here!" She was settling up with a woman at the shoe and sandal stall when she heard a voice from behind her. Sebastian greeted her with a kiss on both cheeks. "I was coming to the hotel to pick you up in an hour."

"Yes, that's right. I just needed to buy some emergency footwear."

Sebastian chatted to the smallholder in Greek, who responded with smiles and nods, then grasped Ella's hand and shook it before they took their leave.

"I better get back." Sebastian glanced over at his stall. "I'll meet you at the hotel later."

Kitten wasn't on duty when they checked into Twin Pines. Ella dumped her bag on the bed and went through the connecting door to her friend's room.

Louise examined her new sandals in the mirror and made sure the strapping looked even. Ella lay on Louise's bed.

A full day of meetings awaited them. First, a visit to the co-operative where they would have individual sessions with each artisan and negotiate the shipping schedules for the rest of the year. After that was done, they'd been invited to lunch at the co-operative. Sebastian had arranged some more meetings later in the afternoon after they had a chance to rest.

The temptation to track Aidan down was strong, but Ella resisted. She was here for work; it was essential to build good relationships with all the suppliers they used. She wanted a relationship with Aidan and had made the first, second, and now the third move. But the last time they spoke, he told her he didn't see any future for them. A woman would have to be stupid to think she could change his mind if that's how he really felt.

She'd only tried to make contact again because Amber and Liam encouraged her by telling about how he kept mooning over photos on his phone. What if they were wrong? What if, instead of looking at photos of her, he was looking at pictures of significant finds or something?

She'd have put herself in this position for a man who was admiring shards or arrowheads. It didn't bear thinking about.

"Thank you." Louise accepted two more ouzotinis from the waitress. She glanced up at the stage area at the front of the bar and couldn't hold back a grimace when the duet screeched a particularly off-key note. "They are brutal. I'm telling you we would do much better."

"What are you thinking? Kylie? Abba? Beatles? There's no way I'm doing Queen again." It had been years ago, back when they first met at a stuffy party for employees of her father's business. The *disgraceful incident* was still a raw memory. Her parents had insisted she attend. Looking back, it was probably a ruse to introduce her to Jason, her father's up and coming junior executive.

Louise had been brought along as another executive's date. They connected instantly behind the scenes in the restroom when Louise asked her for a light. Ella only smoked occasionally back then, so Louise cadged a light from another woman.

"Want one?" She'd shaken the packet in Ella's direction, and they sneaked out the back door into the darkness. They claimed a bench around the side of the building, and for the first time since she left Ireland, Ella found someone she could talk to.

They hadn't managed to leave together. Louise had gone with the executive, who she declined to date again. Ella dutifully returned to her parents' group of potential new best friends and suitors. But before they left that bench, they'd swapped numbers, and within a week, they were meeting for coffee.

The week after that, after way too many vodka tonics, they attempted "Bohemian Rhapsody" in a bijoux club downtown. The memory still made them both laugh. Rather than be booed offstage, the crowd embraced the effort, and the entire bar decided to sing along. Somehow, Louise managed to divide the audience into segments singing different song sections. They finished up to thunderous applause.

Louise shook her head with a grin. "I'd never try that again. I wonder if they've any Backstreet Boys?"

"Will we walk up to the dig site tomorrow?" Louise looked at Ella cautiously. "Or maybe to Aidan's house?"

It was impossible to hide on an island this size unless you wanted to. They'd been here two days and were due to leave on the ferry tomorrow night. Kitten knew they had checked in, and they'd even bumped into her in the hotel lobby this morning. She was welcoming and charming, but in the way that a hotel owner would be to a guest. Nothing more personal than that. She avoided mentioning Nick or Aidan, and couldn't escape quickly enough.

"He must know I'm here." She swallowed a mouthful of her ouzotini.

"You called. You left a message. Kitten will have told her boyfriend, and he will have informed Aidan. To be honest, honey, I know you want him, but if he doesn't have the guts to come to the hotel and find you—" Her face screwed up in a you-know-he's-not-worth-it grimace.

"You're right." It was over. For her own sanity, she needed to accept the truth and let it go. There was no point in door-stepping him at work or ambushing him at home. Anything he could say in reaction to her presence would be, at best, insincere and, at worse, devastating. But if she didn't go—if she left the island without speaking to him—she would always wonder. Twenty years ago, she left without a word. She didn't have a choice in the matter, but she still left. She blamed the loss of her phone and his number for not getting in touch, but insecurity dictated her response. Her fear that he wasn't in love made her believe that he'd received her message and decided not to pursue their relationship. Fear of the unknown stopped her from hunting him down to discover the truth.

Would she do the same thing again? Would she let fear obliterate any slim chance of happiness?

She drained her drink. Caught the waiter's eye and swirled her finger over their empty glasses in the universal another round gesture.

Which is how, an hour later, she and Louise were both on stage singing 'I Want it That Way' and accompanying their performance with some very dodgy dancing. It didn't matter that the audience paid no attention. Or that Louise's down-pointing finger guns move looked ridiculous. She surrendered to the now. The pure joy of giving it one-hundred-percent and making a memory with her best friend filled Ella with happiness.

The future? She'd decide tomorrow.

# Chapter Eighteen

Aidan gazed into his wife's face. He propped his phone up against the lamp on his bedside table and ran his hands through his hair, as he had multiple times since he'd woken.

"I loved you."

Carol's smile didn't waver.

"You didn't do it, did you? You wouldn't."

Carol's smile was fixed.

He sat up in bed. Swung his legs out to plant his feet on the floor. "I'm losing it." Ignoring Carol's picture on his phone, he dressed and walked into the kitchen. The house was quiet. Liam and Nick had left for the dig without him.

Three dirty glasses and an empty bottle of whiskey sat next to the sink.

He poured himself some coffee and walked out onto the patio.

He sat at the table. Cast a glance over to the empty seat where Ella sat mere weeks ago. A black wave welled up in his chest, overwhelming any good memories and suffocating happiness. Kitten and Nick had visited last night and wouldn't leave, even when he shut down and refused to discuss Ella with them.

Nick told him again that he was an idiot. But Kitten took a different approach. He'd had the impression she didn't like Ella much, but she'd been impressed that Ella had returned.

"She asked me about you today. She said she hadn't been able to make contact. That she thinks her messages haven't got through. She wanted to check you were on the island and were okay."

Aidan rubbed the back of his neck. "I'm sorry. I didn't want to involve you—"

"Well, you have." Kitten crossed her arms. "She's a decent woman. Why would you ghost her?"

"I'm not." He clenched his teeth so tight his jaw hurt.

"You got her messages." It wasn't a question, even though she couldn't possibly know if Aidan received Ella's messages or not. "Your phone rang, and you ignored it. Didn't you?"

He swigged a mouthful of whiskey. "Maybe it did. Maybe I did. It doesn't matter."

Kitten's eyes blazed. She snorted, indignant. "I... I'm..."

Nick placed a hand on her arm, holding her in check. "It's a dick move, man. And it's not like you."

"I told her you were on island. And that when I received her reservation, I told you the dates she would be here. She held it together. She straightened her spine and forced a wobbly smile, but her friend clasped her arm as they walked out. Ella didn't ask for support, but she needed it. I can't believe you're the sort of man who would hurt a woman like that."

She stood. "I don't think I can do this, Nick. I'm so angry I fear I'll make things worse, not better." She fired off a quick text. "I've asked my brother to give me a lift home on his motorbike."

She walked to the door, and Nick hurried after her. Aidan poured himself another.

They were too distant for him to make out any words, but their body language was clear. Kitten was waving her arms around and even at one point stamped a foot. Nick was trying to calm her down, trying to explain, trying to make allowances for him.

Jesus. Kitten was right. What sort of a low-life had he become?

After she left in a cloud of black exhaust fumes, he tried to explain.

Nick talked about his life with Kitten. How he'd been scared, at first, to take the chance, but how he didn't regret one minute of the time they'd been together. He coaxed and cajoled Aidan to grab the opportunity and talk to Ella, who would be leaving on the evening ferry the next night.

"It's better if I don't see her. I told her there was no future for us. She knows what will happen if she just turns up." Disgust roiled through him as he spoke the words. They were evasive and cowardly, and both of them knew it. "She may be hurt now, but she'll heal quicker if she hates me."

Nick had grimaced. "The sad thing is, I think you've even persuaded yourself to believe the shit you're spouting."

That had been the final nail in the coffin of their conversation. Aidan started talking about the dig on Akrotiri, and Nick, defeated, surrendered. Aidan kept the conversation away from his love life through dogged determination. A couple of hours before dawn, Nick settled on the sofa, and Aidan slinked off to bed.

He'd asked Nick to let him sleep and take Liam to the dig the following day. The only person's company he could bear today was his own.

He rubbed a hand over his scratchy jawline. He should

shower. Shave. Get a grip on his life rather than falling to pieces. He drained his coffee.

Then the doorbell rang.

* * *

There were swirls in the wood grain of the front door. Ella pushed her hands together and forced herself to stay still. Which was more difficult than she thought it would be. She presented a calm surface, but inside, everything was rioting to flee.

She'd rung the bell. She set this confrontation in motion, and there was no escaping.

This morning over breakfast, she explained to Louise how she felt. It had been difficult to formulate the words, but once she had, Louise understood.

She had been concerned but supportive.

So now she stood on the doorstep. Waiting for rejection, but this time in person.

Her throat moved. Her fingers squeezed tight. If Aidan were here, the door wouldn't be locked. She could push against it. She clamped her eyes shut.

And opened them the moment she heard the door open.

Shock flickered in Aidan's eyes before he locked it down. The look of surprise became a frown. His hair was mussed, and his five o'clock shadow was closer to a dark midnight almost-beard. "You're here." He sounded as though he couldn't believe the evidence of his eyes.

"Yes." Her heart hammered. She glanced past him into the cool interior. "Can I come in?"

For a moment, it seemed as though he might refuse. But then he opened the door wider and angled away to let her enter. A thousand butterflies took flight in her gut when she walked past him and down the corridor to the kitchen. She'd second-guessed herself all night. Had almost persuaded herself she didn't deserve an answer—didn't need to know. Then she thought of the future. Of what she'd say to herself years hence when she thought back to this summer. Would she rewrite history to make it sound better to her own ears like she had twenty years ago?

He walked past her and sat in the old armchair by the fire. His eyes were narrowed, and his jaw clenched like he was in pain. Instead of leaning back in the chair, he hunched forward and rested his forearms on his knees. "You gonna sit down?"

It was an invitation—a reluctant one, but still an invitation. Ella perched on the edge of the sofa and made eye contact. "I want to know what changed."

He scowled. Leaned back and crossed his arms. "I just came to my senses, that's all."

"Bullshit." Poisonous insecurity sat on her shoulder and whispered, *you're not good enough*, in her ear, but she mentally flicked it off. "You held me in your arms and told me you'd miss me on the quay in Kosmima. You meant it." She caught the flick of heat in the depths of his eyes before he looked away.

"Aidan. You care about me. Just like I care about you. Like I've always cared about you." She stood and walked over to stand in front of him. "I didn't fight for you back then. I believed my parents when they told me I disgraced the family and that I should be ashamed. I blamed everyone except myself for losing you. My parents for rushing me out of the country. My father for insisting I dump all social media. My mother for taking my phone so I couldn't call you. Even a stranger for not passing on my quickly scrawled letter with my address."

Aidan's shoulders stiffened.

"But the truth was, I didn't fight any of it. I could have found your address. Could have found your number and called, but I didn't. I let it go. I let us go." She placed her hands on his shoulders. "I won't make that mistake again. I know you have feelings for me. I want you back."

He stood, stepped sideways, so her hands fell away. There was a sadness in his eyes mixed with something else, maybe regret or its ugly cousin, pity.

"I wish you hadn't come here today." He rubbed the back of his neck. "I don't want to hurt you."

Every word, every look, pierced like a knife.

"But?" Her voice sounded raspy.

"We don't have a future." He glanced at the doorway. "I can give you a lift back into the village."

"No." She walked close and stared up into his face, desperate to penetrate his inscrutable expression. "I need more. I care about you. I want to be with you."

He screwed his eyes tight. His hands curled into fists. "Ella, just leave it."

"No." She pressed her hand to his chest. His heartbeat raced under her palm. "Tell me. Tell me why."

His eyes opened. Warring emotions were evident in their depths. Desire, anger, regret. Then back to desire. With a muffled curse, he cupped the back of her neck and pulled her close. Then he covered her mouth with his own and kissed her passionately.

The fire that flared to life in an instant was extinguished just as rapidly. He grasped her shoulders and moved her away. "We had fun. That's all it was ever supposed to be." His expression was harsh and unyielding. As if the moments they spent kissing had been some aberration he'd already forgotten.

He was right. This was only ever meant to be a fun capsule of time. One that would be over once Liam and Amber arrived on the island. Somewhere along the way, she'd let it mean more. And had been stupid enough to believe he felt the same. She'd misread all the signals because she wanted more. When he said he would miss her, she read more into his bland statement; painted it with a deeper meaning that he hadn't intended.

He touched her face, wiping away tears. "Don't cry." His frown deepened, and his mouth twisted. "Don't cry, Ella."

Controlling her body's reaction to his rejection was impossible. Once upon a time, she would have tried, but now she surrendered to the pain. "Could you drive me back to the taverna?"

"I'll get my keys."

She watched his departing back for a moment. Then blinked away the tears and blew out a breath through shaking lips.

* * *

"You look absolutely shite, Aidan." Siobhan peered at her brother as though he was something nasty she tracked into the house on the bottom of her shoe. "What happened to you?"

She inspected him up and down. "You've lost weight. You need a haircut. How long has it been since you shaved?"

His sister had always been a pain in the ass. "You're looking great, too." Ironically, she actually did. She was usually too busy carrying kids around to bother with make-up or dressing in anything other than sweats. But today, her pale eyelashes were darkened with mascara, and he was pretty sure he could make out a trace of lipstick on her lips. She wore midnight blue jeans and a pale pink shirt open at the neck to show off a thick gold chain, and matching dangly gold earrings hung from her ear lobes. "Something's different about your hair."

She touched the side of her head. "I got highlights. And a curly blow-dry." She went pink. "It's a special day."

It didn't feel special. It felt like another bloody dark day to survive living through, just like every day since he returned to Dublin.

He loved working on Kosmima every summer. The charge injected into his life was usually enough to buoy him up for his return to Ireland. In the past, he packed away the joy of working on the island dig with his summer clothes, and squashed any traces of dissatisfaction that colored his Dublin lecturing job. He usually shrugged off discontent and knuckled down to work. But now, things were different.

Long forgotten ghosts accompanied him as he walked around the college. From the corner of his eye, he kept imagining he saw her, both as she had been twenty years ago and as she was now. Breaking off all communication had worked in that he hadn't spoken to her since that day six weeks ago. But flushing her from his thoughts, erasing her from his memories, and dissolving the hard stone of want for her in his chest was a different matter.

She was in his mind when he woke every morning.

The last thought in his head as he lay in bed every night.

He forced himself to focus on his sister. "Why's it such a special day?"

She tapped her wedding ring with a painted fingernail. "Wedding anniversary. Mam's looking after the kids, and Joe and I are going away overnight!" She emphasized the last word with a grin and a wiggling happy dance. "Overnight! Just the two of us."

Being the parent of a toddler and a preschooler was just a distant memory, but his sister's enthusiasm was infectious. He shook his head ruefully. "I don't know how you have the energy to chase after them. What time are you leaving?"

"Joe went into the office to just finish up some paperwork. He's meeting me here in forty minutes." She flicked on the kettle and took down mugs from the cupboard over the sink. "I came over to see if you're as bad as everyone says you are."

She spooned instant coffee into the mugs. Slanted him a look.

"Who has been saying—"

"Who hasn't, more like. Mam's worried about you. Liam says you've been mooning about since your romance went south. Nick even called me and asked me to pop in and check on you." She glowered at him. "Don't roll your eyes at me." She made the coffee and slid a mug across the table to him. "You need to tell me what's the matter." She looked at her watch. "You've half an hour. Spill."

Siobhan was the only one who knew the entire story. They'd always been close. He'd asked her to be there for the weekend he would bring Ella to meet his parents. The first time he brought a girl home was bound to be whipped up into a big deal, and having Siobhan there would diffuse the effect of his mother's over-excited response.

Siobhan had seen the devastation firsthand when he told her his girlfriend would not be coming for a visit—that he didn't have a girlfriend any longer, or didn't think he did.

Once he started talking, it became apparent that Siobhan knew much of what had happened over the summer. She'd always been great at digging deep and uncovering secrets. No one could say no to Siobhan.

"Nick likes her." She tilted her head to the side and fixed him with her most penetrating stare. "He went out of his way to tell me that. Nick normally doesn't interfere in your love life, but he was adamant that you and she were good together." She chewed a biscuit. "I told him I didn't like how she elbowed her way back into your life, that I didn't think she deserved a second chance, but he didn't agree."

"Nick doesn't know everything."

"What doesn't he know?" She scowled. "I can't believe she dumped you again. Is she with someone else? I swear, that b—"

"She's not a bitch. She didn't dump me. I ended things." He rubbed the ache over his heart. "She had to leave in a hurry. We spoke on the phone a couple of times and decided it was over, but she came back to the island and asked for another chance."

Siobhan's eyes widened. Her head tilted. "Ballsy." She considered for a moment. "Wait—did you both decide it was over, or did you decide that on your own?"

"I decided." And it was a decision that tormented him ever since.

She glanced at her watch again. Drained her coffee cup. "Why?"

He had no answer.

His sister leaned forward across the table. "Aidan? I don't understand. You're miserable. Everyone can see it. Liam and Nick said you were happy. Why the hell would you self-sabotage?"

"We live in different countries, we— Oh, fuck it." There wasn't any excuse he could give that would make sense, except the truth. "Liam and I discovered that Carol and Ella were in the same society in college."

Parallel lines between Siobhan's eyes pulled together. "Liam showed me the photo on his phone. So what?"

"So, Ella told me she didn't leave without a word. She gave a note to someone—and that person might have been Carol." There was a sour taste in his mouth. Loathing crawled under his skin at the suspicions that had plagued him since seeing the picture. "What if Carol destroyed it? What if she wanted to take Ella's place in my life?" He rubbed his eyes. "I don't want to think like this. I don't want to suspect Carol of doing something like that. She called Trouble *the one that got away*. If me being with Ella was something Carol didn't want, how can I even think of a future with her?"

The doorbell rang.

Siobhan stood. "Hold that thought." She opened the door to her husband and talked to him quickly on the doorstep. Joe trekked back to the car.

"You should go." Aidan stood.

"Sit your ass back down, little brother."

# Chapter Nineteen

Sunlight flooded the scene at the Silver Stars craft festival at the Monterey County Fairgrounds. Ella and Louise were taking five at a tiny metal table in front of Carl's Coffee Roasters and sampling the merchandise.

Louise glanced over at the *Precious Things* Collective's range of stalls. The sun had brought out the shoppers. Parents pushed buggies as they browsed. Kids and adults alike clustered around the fresh pancake stall, and at the Collective's booths, the artisans chatted with the shoppers as they made sales.

"Business is good," Louise said.

"It's great." Some of the craftspeople had attended the craft festival in previous years, but this was their first foray into direct selling. Mark Malthus, an enthusiastic and talented potter in his thirties, had taken Concha Fernandez under his wing and was reminding her how to use the card swipe app on her phone. People thronged to Concha's stall, not just for the beautiful lace she worked, but also to meet the woman whose work had been featured on the 'what's on this weekend' section this Friday night.

It wasn't every day you saw a ninety-six-year-old artisan manning a stall.

Concha was a marketing genius. She'd asked Mark to spill out his wares onto her table, too. Every person who came over to browse ended up chatting with the old lady about lacemaking. And when they were ready to move on, she introduced them to her neighbor and raved over his beautiful pottery. It was a truly symbiotic relationship.

"Concha's not getting too tired, is she?" Ella checked her watch. "She's been here for a couple of hours, and she was here yesterday, too."

"Her daughter and granddaughter are walking around. Sara will take over the stall while her mother drives Concha home to rest."

The words had barely left Louise's lips before the two women arrived to relieve the old lady. Mark greeted Sara, who seemed to blush as they chatted.

"Sparks?" Louise had noticed, too.

"He asked me earlier if Sara would be coming back today." Mark was smitten, and it seemed as if Sara felt the same.

Ella felt like that once.

A melancholy ache filled her chest at the sudden unwelcome thought of Aidan.

Her phone buzzed on the table. She picked it up. Aidan. Again.

She rejected the call. Placed the phone face-side down.

Carl was strolling past and stopped. "Can I get you ladies more coffee? Maybe a slice of chocolate cake?"

A slab of cake might take the edge off. "Yes. Definitely. For both of us." Ella handed over a twenty and drained the dregs of her coffee. "Thanks, Carl."

Louise tapped Ella's phone with a long scarlet fingernail. "Him again?"

Ella nodded. "He's called me every day for the past two

weeks." She rubbed the back of her neck. "He texts too, but I haven't read them."

"Aren't you curious?" Louise tilted her head to the side in the way she always did when she was dying to know more. "Maybe he's come to his senses."

"Too little, too late." She crossed her arms and refused to think of him. "He hurt me, Lou. You saw me when I came back from his house. I was a wreck. I more than put myself out there; I prostrated myself at his feet and begged him to love me. I'm done with that now."

"But don't you even want to know why he's calling?"

Louise beamed a megawatt smile at Carl, who almost tripped while carrying their order. Bearded baristas were a favorite of hers.

"I don't." If she did, she could read his messages. Once or twice she'd been tempted. Until she remembered their last meeting and let herself feel the full flood of the painful emotions again. She was brave, but she wasn't a masochist.

He didn't want to be seen as the bad guy. She could understand that. And they'd never promised anything to each other. They'd been clear that their romance was a temporary thing, but somewhere along the way everything had changed.

Amber and Liam's relationship had downshifted to friends.

They wanted their parents to be happy, and they had no compunction about trying to help. Which meant Ella had been bombarded with 'Liam says...' updates about Aidan's mood for a full couple of weeks after she returned from Kosmima. Amber was hard-headed. She paid little notice to Ella's hints that she didn't want to hear about Aidan. Had kept matchmaking and scheming until Ella snapped and told her it was hopeless. That it was over.

"I never thought you were a coward." Louise's face was deadpan. She might have been joking, or maybe not.

"I'm just...I just..." Ella snatched up the phone and examined it. "Fourteen messages and twenty texts." Her stomach churned.

"May I?" Louise took the phone. "I could listen to the messages and tell you what they say. It might be easier than hearing his voice."

"Fine." Her instinct was to avoid hearing—even secondhand—whatever Aidan had to say. She didn't need another friend. She needed more than that. And more was no longer an option for the two of them.

Louise pressed the phone to her ear and listened. At the beginning of his message, her expression was impassive, but a slow smile was on her face by the end.

"What?"

"He asked you to answer his call and said he needs to talk. He's sorry about screwing up that day on Kosmima. He wants to explain why." She smiled. "And then he said he wants to remind you of the fun times you had together. He asked you to remember Bloomsday. And how instead of dressing in Edwardian Costume to celebrate Ulysses, you went on a pub crawl dressed as Ariel and Prince Eric."

Ella hadn't forgotten, but the memory had been deeply suppressed and not thought of for years.

"Seriously?" Louise's expression was incredulous.

Ella laughed. "Tail, long red curly wig, and everything. I had to hop along the road. Aidan looked fantastic in an open-necked flowing white shirt, tight black trousers, and pirate boots. I just heard pub crawl and fancy dress and went with my gut." The night had been so much fun. Everywhere they went, people gave Aidan a double-take but snorted with laughter the moment they caught sight of her long green tail or her seashell bra.

"Could you listen to the next message?"

* * *

Louise listened to the next message. When she finished, she handed the phone back. "He asks you again to answer your phone when he calls. Says he needs to hear your voice. And then he shared another memory." She fiddled with the clasp of her bag. "I don't want to listen to the messages anymore. He's pouring out his heart with those memories. It feels wrong for anyone but you to be listening."

What the hell had he said? Ella grimaced.

Louise shook her head. "No. No. I don't mean they're x-rated. He talked about when you were in college. One night he was late to meet you in the bar, and you'd left. He went to your accommodation, and you refused to let him in."

"And he serenaded me." It had been impossible to stay cross as he stood under her window and hammed it up, pouring out his heart while clutching his chest.

"He said you finally relented and let him in to stop your neighbors complaining."

"Yes." She couldn't stop smiling. He'd been contrite, charming, and kissed her so wildly she had forgiven him the moment his lips met hers. "I should listen."

Louise nodded. "You should listen."

She went out to the parking lot and slid behind the wheel.

Nearby, people walked and talked. The cars left and right were empty, and no one noticed her sitting alone and unmoving. She placed the phone on the dashboard and set it on speaker.

Aidan's voice filled the cab, so clear it was almost as if he were there beside her. "I'll keep calling. I'll call you every day until you answer and talk to me."

Tiny hairs stood up on the back of her neck at his bluntly honest words.

"Do you remember how you got that nickname? I do." He

paused for a moment. "My sister reminded me the last time I saw her here in Dublin. She never met you, but she christened you Trouble because of the effect you had on me. I told her how I bailed on going to football with my mates one Saturday, and they teased me for being under your control. I told Siobhan I wanted to go to brunch with you rather than kick a ball around with them. She teased me for having a crush, and I told her it was no crush, that I was in love. Her reply? 'You missed football to have brunch with a girl? She sounds like trouble.'"

The message ended. Ella sat for a long moment, remembering. She hadn't known the origin of her nickname; he just started calling her Trouble one day, and before she knew it, everyone followed suit. It had been early in their relationship, and the fact that he felt so strongly that he'd told his sister he was in love was unexpected. At that stage, she just buzzed with electricity every time they met. Every time they kissed.

Reminiscing about how they'd been twenty years ago was all very well, but what relevance did it have to the people they were today? She'd thought their connection had been re-established—that he felt the same—when they spent time together on the island. But he let her leave without making any attempt to stop her even when she begged for a second chance.

Anger, bitterness, and a residual sadness struggled for dominance, but weak hope and a desire to hear the other messages won out. Ella pulled her sweater cuffs down over her hands and listened to another message.

"I never wanted you to be any more than a memory." Aidan's voice was quiet and serious. "Because, for the most part, you were a good memory. The times I had with you were unlike any time I had with anyone else in my life. We had a closeness and a connection that felt bone-deep. After you left, I didn't want to think of you. I erased the memories of being with you. Or at least, I thought I did."

Outside the window, it started to rain. Ella watched the trail of water weave down the side window. It meandered like a miniature river, joining up with any single raindrops suspended on the glass's surface.

"When you walked into the taverna, everything changed. When your eyes met mine, a surge of electricity brought me alive. I fought it. I didn't think about how I reacted then. I've had plenty of time to think about it since. I tried to deny the attraction because I didn't want to get hurt."

He made a noise that was part sigh, part self-aware laugh.

"Talking to you like this is strange. I guess this must be what talking to a therapist is like. I'm opening up and making myself vulnerable, and I don't even know if you're getting these messages."

The raindrop met an invisible spot of resistance and diverted at a ninety-degree angle before wandering down the window again. Ella pressed her finger to the glass.

"What I'm trying to say is that I didn't want to fall in love with you again. My heart couldn't take it. You kept saying that the time we had was limited, and you were right. I live on one side of the world and you on the other. But being with you, day after day, eating dinner opposite you in the taverna, made me want to try. Because the night I went for dinner, and you weren't there, it was as though the light bled out of my world. I sat facing the door and waited until the last possible moment to order because I was holding out hope you would walk through it. I can't choose to love or not love you. Loving you isn't a choice. It's just part of who I am."

"So why did you push me away when I came back to the island?" Ella spoke aloud in the cocoon of the car.

"Call me back." The message ended.

She closed her eyes. There were still many messages to listen to and texts to read, but being drip-fed these fragments drove her insane. She understood how Aidan felt vulnerable opening up to her. She'd felt the same when she warred with herself on Kosmima, wondering if she dared to go and ask him for a second chance. It had taken all she had to knock on his door and ask to come in.

Now he was asking her to take the same leap again.

Loving you isn't a choice.

It didn't feel like a choice for her either. One minute it was joy, the next agony. But she couldn't choose to love him because loving him was a reality.

She could live it.

# Chapter Twenty

She called. She eventually called. Aidan had almost given up hope that she would. A normal person might have cut their losses and surrendered. They might have chosen not to put themselves through any more agony of waiting and blocked her from their cell phone and their thoughts.

But as he'd said, there was no choice involved for him. He just loved Ella, plain and simple. That wouldn't change if she didn't love him back or wasn't willing to try again; he'd still love her. If they would never be together, he'd just have to live with it. He'd be able to push the memories down, rebuild the wall between memories of Ella and the rest of his world. He knew that because he'd done it before.

How were women just such different creatures?

It had taken a discussion with Siobhan to rip the mask away from his eyes. She asked him a series of questions:

"Do you love her?"

He'd tried to avoid that one. Had explained that it wasn't that simple, but his sister had brought him right back to the question and refused to let him off the hook until he admitted, yes, he did.

"What's your number one reason for not being with her?"

He'd stumbled through an ill-thought-out ramble. Maybe Carol kept them apart. How could he feel anger and resentment to the woman he'd loved and had a child with if that was the case? After Carol's death, Siobhan and every other person who cared about him said, "She'd want you to be happy. She'd want you to find someone else."

But Carol had known Ella. If she had that letter and not passed it on, it was because she hadn't wanted them to be together. She would have wanted him to be happy. He knew that. But maybe she wouldn't have wanted him to be happy with the woman she called 'the one that got away.' Especially not if she'd been instrumental in ensuring the one that got away stayed away.

Siobhan had given him the look. The same look she'd given him all their lives since they were little children.

"Firstly, your reasoning is so screwed up I can't even...." She rubbed her eyebrow. "You loved Carol. And she loved you. You have to deal with what you know. With facts. And the facts of the matter are that you were in love and you produced a beautiful child together.

"Secondly, you've forgotten. I was the one who called Ella 'the one that got away' first. I was so angry about how she treated you that I started referring to her that way because it was less bitter than the way I wanted to refer to her. Carol picked it up from me."

She placed both of her hands over his on the table. "And thirdly, you have no reason to think Ella gave the note to Carol—bar a photograph showing that they were in the same society. It's highly unlikely that Carol was the one she talked to that day. And you probably will never know if she did or not. And does it matter?"

"Of course it matters."

"Why? Would you love Carol any less?" Before he had a chance to form a reply, she continued. "You wouldn't. I know Carol. She loved you with everything she had, and you were a great husband who loved her back. If you died instead of her, would you have any reservations about her finding somebody to love?"

He'd done enough talking. Had stripped open his chest to reveal his vulnerable, beating heart. So when Ella finally called, he didn't want to waste any more time.

"I've listened to some of your messages." She sounded hesitant. "I think we need to talk."

"I agree." He climbed into his car and started the engine. "I'll meet you at your beach house tomorrow."

Not knowing what he meant was driving Ella crazy. Was he flying in from Ireland, or was he in America already? Aidan terminated the call before she had a chance to ask. She resisted the temptation to call him back or to text. She'd know the answer in a day. So after the call, she made her way back to the stalls and confided everything in Louise. Amber was spending the night with a friend and wasn't due back until the evening, so they would have privacy to talk. All she had to do was wait.

The sun was up early, and so was she.

She cleaned the house. Next, she laid out multiple outfits on the bed and drank three cups of coffee. She checked her phone.

When she found herself straightening the chairs in the breakfast nook for the third time, it became clear that waiting was shredding her composure and setting her nerves on full alert. Aidan hadn't specified a time. It could be hours before he would arrive.

She needed to decompress. And the perfect solution was right outside her window, sparkling turquoise in the early-morning sunlight.

She strode into the bedroom to change into her brand-new rainbow stripe bikini and pulled on a tee-shirt over the top. Then she walked out of her back door, picked up her surfboard, and ran into the sea.

It was not a good day for surfing. The water was dead calm with soft waves. Ella left her surfboard on the beach and swam for a while, then retrieved it and paddled out into the blue. She lay on the board, fingers trailing in the clear water, watching the beach.

The tight clutch of panicked anticipation in her chest had eased with all the physical activity. But still, she wanted to avoid sitting inside waiting for his arrival.

The sun beat down, drying the tee-shirt to her back. She felt its heat on the back of her legs. She should go inside. Shower. Wash and dry her hair. But still, she didn't move. The board was warm against the side of her face. Little waves slapped and kissed the side of the board, so close to her face if she shifted a fraction, they would splash her.

What time is it? Maybe he'd phoned. Maybe he had come to her front door, not received a response, and left. Surely he'd check the beach.

She shifted position on the board and paddled to shore.

* * *

Her car was outside the house. And the blinds were up. But there was no answer when he rang the doorbell, and there was no sign of life through the windows.

Aidan found a path along the side of the houses that led to the beach and started down it. He called her number and pressed the phone to his ear as he walked. It rang, but she didn't pick up.

The reason became clear as he passed the houses to the beach.

The dry sand shifted under his feet, impossible to walk on in shoes. One solitary person was in view, paddling on a surfboard to shore. He recognized her immediately, even at a distance.

Of course she'd be on the water.

He took off his shoes and walked to her.

She was almost at the shore by the time he reached her. The board floated just out of arm's reach.

"Hi." There was distrust in the depths of her eyes. A distrust he'd put there.

He took in every inch of her. Tousled, wet hair, long tanned legs. A flash of rainbow bikini bottoms. And a tee-shirt. He frowned as he peered closer. Ricky Martin.

She looked down.

"Is that..."

She smiled. "I just put on the nearest tee-shirt. I didn't even realize it was this one."

"My tee-shirt. From the concert." It was more than that. It was the first and only gift he'd ever given her. And the cause of their separation. "I haven't seen that since you lifted it to flash me. I'm amazed you still have it."

The waves brought the board closer, inch by inch.

He walked into the waves, knee-deep.

Her eyes widened, and the small smile bloomed into a full one. "You're getting soaked."

"I am." He reached the board. She sat on it, with her legs dangling into the water.

"You're crazy." He nodded. "Guilty. Crazy for letting you go. Crazy for thinking that I didn't deserve a future with you.

Crazy for risking a chance at happiness." He trailed his fingers down her arm. "Crazy about you."

"I don't know how you're here."

He looked surprised. "You didn't hear my message?"

"I didn't hear many of your messages. Or read many of your texts. I was ignoring you. I only started listening to them yesterday."

Residual hurt was evident in her expression.

"In that case, I'll have to tell you everything." He wanted to pull her from that surfboard. Tear off her wet tee-shirt and wrap his arms around her. But first, they had to talk. He had to explain.

"Let's go inside." She glanced at his soaked jeans. "You'll have to strip and wrap yourself in a towel."

He had a suitcase in the car. So he changed while Ella showered.

He fixed coffee and sat at the tiny kitchen table waiting for her.

She came out wrapped in a robe with her towel-dried hair tumbling around her shoulders.

"You're beautiful."

"Thank you." She poured a cup of coffee and added sugar.

"You knew my wife, Carol." He didn't want to know the truth. Had struggled with the idea of never mentioning their connection and letting it go. Siobhan's suggestion had probably been intelligent, but he couldn't bear starting a new life with the question hovering in the background.

"What?" Ella screwed up her face. "I didn't know your wife."

"You did. At Trinity."

She drank a slug of coffee. Shook her head. "I don't remember anyone called Carol." She shot him a glance. "How do you know I knew her? You never mentioned this before."

"Liam worked it out. He found an old photo." He took out his phone and flicked through the picture roll till he located the photograph. Then he placed it on the counter in front of her.

"You." He pointed at her familiar features. "Carol." A different row, another familiar face.

She scrutinized it, zooming in to see more detail. "Camera Society." She looked up into his eyes. "I joined every society in college that first semester. Mom told me it was the best way to make friends." She zoomed in to look at Carol's face. "I don't think I went to more than two of their meetings. I don't remember ever seeing her." Her expression softened. "She was very pretty."

Aidan looked away.

"Aidan."

He focused on Ella again. "When I saw this picture, I thought maybe you'd known each other back then. That she might have been the person you gave the letter to."

"No!" Ella was adamant. "I gave the letter to a girl called Pippa. I remember her, but I don't remember meeting Carol. We must have occupied the same space for the photograph, but that's all. So you thought Carol might have had the letter?"

"I didn't want to think so, but I had to consider it. Liam showed me the photograph just after you left. I was still struggling with the implications when you came back. I couldn't see what was important. I'm sorry I hurt you." He stared into her eyes. The eyes that he hoped to stare into every morning going forward.

"What changed?" She caught the side of her bottom lip in her teeth. "You started calling and texting, still thinking that Carol may have destroyed my letter. What happened to change your mind about us?"

"Siobhan happened."

Unable to resist touching her, he reached for her hand. He

rubbed his thumb over her soft skin as the last fragment of their story slotted into place. "She made me see that it didn't matter what had happened in either of our pasts. That all we have is now and the hope of a future. And I want to spend my now with you. I don't want to take it slow or see how it goes. I want to be with you. One hundred percent all-in."

Her eyes shone. "I want that, too."

"I've taken up a guest lecturer position at Monterey U. I'll be here for the next semester. We can work out the rest later." He stood and pulled her up into his arms. "I love you."

Her body pressed against his. "I love you, too," she whispered against his mouth a second before they kissed.

Everyone had trouble in their lives—now he had his.

# Chapter Twenty-One

DECEMBER 24TH

"Everyone is waiting for their desserts."

Aidan swept Ella's hair back to kiss her neck from behind. His hands snaked around her waist. "They're fine."

She leaned back against his firm chest and felt her insides melt. They hadn't spent a day apart since he strode out into the ocean fully dressed to join her. Slotting their complicated lives together hadn't been easy, but they were making it work. Minute by minute. Day by day.

"Your mother will come and investigate." She swiveled in his arms, touched the sides of his face, and pressed a quick kiss against his mouth. "And I don't want to be caught in the act again."

"Because that would be disgraceful." His mother had walked in on them kissing in the kitchen a couple of days ago. She'd waved her hands in the air and dashed out. It wasn't as though either of them had shed any clothes, but she'd huffed as though they were in flagrante delicto.

Ella stepped back. She grabbed a plate from the counter

and pushed it into his hands. "You take the apple pie and ice cream, and I'll bring the banoffee."

They returned to the dining room. Luckily, it looked as though Aidan was right; their blended families had been too busy talking to notice their absence.

Siobhan's attempt to feed healthy food to her children had to be abandoned when they noticed the puddings. Aidan's mother was busy advising Amber on the foolproof way to apply lipstick. She was smearing it liberally on her lips, kissing pieces of tissue, and then putting on another coat.

Amber followed suit. Liam could barely hold back laughter as he watched them across the table.

Tomorrow would be a smaller affair. Jason and Betsy had decided to spend the holidays in Dublin and host Christmas dinner at their rented apartment. Amber would join them, and they'd bring her back to America to stay with them until the new year.

Liam, Aidan, and Ella were invited to Siobhan's.

A new year meant a new semester in Dublin for Amber. A new term back in Ireland for Aidan and Ella was starting a new chapter, too.

Ella and Louise had taken on an employee to deal with website orders for *Precious Things*, and the business ran like clockwork with little input from either of them. Louise ran operations from the States, and Ella was now their international buyer.

Ella was open to new experiences and new challenges.

While on Kosmima, she'd spent time talking to Betty about her qualifications and had been amazed to discover that Betty had no formal training for the job she did at the dig every summer. A basic grounding, topped up with short courses to keep up to date with new advances and plenty of experience, was all she needed.

Ella had decided to follow in her friend's footsteps and get some more training before they spent the summer on Kosmima.

She looked across the table at the man who'd stolen her heart so many years ago. His mother was laughing at one of his jokes. He was playing the fool, gesticulating madly—just because it made her laugh more.

Amber was laughing, too.

He turned his attention to her and gave her a wink. Her heart swelled, then overflowed with love.

There were no wedding plans. Not yet. The only plan that mattered was to stay together forever. And enjoy every single moment of the rest of their lives.

THE END

Printed in Great Britain
by Amazon

20244895R00130